BRIAN ZLUTICKY

BULLHEAD
By Brian Zluticky
Copyright © 2021 Brian Zluticky

ALL RIGHTS RESERVED WORLDWIDE

Somewhere in Chinese Occupied America…

ANGP PROMO

1

Your TV fades in on a seedy neighborhood of rundown abandoned houses bordering an industrial park. Bright sunlight casts stark shadows. No one is around. A horn screams as a freight train rumbles across the road two blocks up. A dog barks somewhere.

A cocky twenty-something guy - tall, slender but strong, close-cropped light brown hair, firm jaw, tailored dark suit and skinny tie, cowboy hat and silver-tipped cowboy boots - struts into view. He pulls down the brim of his Stetson, shading his narrow blue eyes, and levels a 12 gauge pump shotgun directly at you.

"You could be America's Next Great Psycho," he says, stern as a lawman. "Jack the Ripper, Norman Bates, the Night Stalker, Hannibal the Cannibal. Just like you, they all started out as closet killers. Come on my TV show and I'll give you the exposure and national attention to make you famous... and then I'll waste your ass."

Fast as lightning he pivots left, fires, and blasts out the

picture window of a nearby shanty. Glass shatters. A distant wailing siren slowly grows louder.

"Hear that? Hear a lot of em these days. Cops are busy. Way too busy. That's where I come in. To sort of," smiling. "Lend a helping hand."

He rests the shotgun back over his shoulder and tips back the brim of his hat.

"Howdy folks, I'm Johnny Wonder. Host of the new hit reality TV show America's Next Great Psycho. Do you feel there's a homicidal maniac hiding in your neighborhood? If you do, then I encourage you to visit us online. There, you'll find a short questionnaire. It'll ask you to list all the strange and creepy things you've been noticing from your person of interest. And, should we find he fits our violent criminal profile... ."

A slender thirty-year-old woman, just a few inches shorter than Johnny, slides into view, slipping her right hand lightly onto his lower back. She's cool in her black designer suit over a hot pink tube top. Dark designer shades, resting high up her narrow nose, contrast starkly with her hollow white cheeks. Her thin red lips are slightly parted, curling at the corners. Her brown tousled pageboy hair is a bit restless in the slight breeze.

"Hi," teeth flashing in the bright sunlight. "I'm Ariadne, Johnny's sidekick and partner in justice. Should your POI meet our profile, look for us to show up in your town for an audition. And, just maybe, you'll get to eyewitness some ANGP-style justice.

The wailing alarm turns a corner and starts getting painfully close.

"None of my contestants," Johnny shouts. "Have lasted longer than 72 hours after their screen test."

He pumps the shotgun and fires it one-handed up at the sun.

"C'mon babe," turning. They both run and hop into a Mustang convertible idling curbside. Ariadne, behind the wheel, peels out, speeding down the deserted street. Johnny, riding shotgun, turns and looks back, flashing razorblade eyes.

"Please do not try to engage these psychos yourselves. Both Ariadne and I are trained professionals in psychology and violent criminal retirement. See you on the streets."

He smiles, pulls down the brim of his hat, and turns back around. The Mustang recedes and vanishes into the shimmering heat waves.

Your screen fades to black.

SAGE & SNAKES

2

Sage Rabnow - a fit fifty-year-old woman with long steel-grey hair, tattoos threatening to overtake her body, and a sharp nose for making a buck - is sitting in her bathrobe at her kitchen table enjoying a hot cup of gourmet coffee and a veggie cream cheese bagel while perusing the morning paper.

Sitting in the chair next to her is Snakes Hardly, her young lover, who had dutifully gone out and procured the coffee and bagel from the Coffee Cabin in downtown Breckenridge. He's all decked out in his grease-stained BROFOs Motorcycle Club gear: motorcycle boots, khaki trousers, navy blue blazer with the sleeves hacked off at the shoulders and the club colors on the back (flaming cross with BROFO above and JESUS LIVES below, both in Gothic). Underneath, he's bare chested. He's just finishing his coffee and replying to a text message he'd just gotten.

All the shades in the cluttered room are drawn to keep out prying eyes. Glints of bright morning light intrude around the edges. The ceiling chandler, on a dimmer switch, glows dull orange.

"Gotta run, hun," Snakes says, admiring her cleavage as he pockets his phone.

Sage folds the paper and tosses it across the table onto a heap of unopened bills.

"Uhhhh," stretching. "And I should get dressed. Got to meet my lawyer."

Snakes scuds his chair back on the linoleum, gets up, goes behind Sage and massages her shoulders. She groans with pleasure. He buries his face in her hair.

"God, I love the smell of sleep on you."

She stands, turns into his embrace, her robe falling open exposing her hot tanned flesh. They kiss deeply.

"Mmmm," Sage breaks the kiss and smiles up into his hungry eyes. "My stud muffin," drops her head onto his strong hairy chest, inhaling the lingering smell of gasoline from his biker vest. "So, today's the day."

"Yup, ma-am," stroking her hair. "Package is just outside of town."

She giggles, "I love it when you get all clandestine on me," clawing the back of his scuzzy trousers. "Can you delay it a few hours? I should clean up this mess, at least offer a show of respectability."

"Think I can manage that," breaking their embrace but taking her hand as he motions toward the house's back door.

"Remember our secret knock."

"Gotcha. Beethoven's Fifth. Two quick taps followed by a soft and a hard. How'd you think of that, anyway?"

Smiling and flashing him devil eyes, "It's how you gave me my first orgasm," squeezing his hand and tugging him to her.

"Now stop that. You're gonna make me haul you back into the bedroom," breathing hot into her face. "I'll be late and we'll blow this whole deal."

"I know," pouting. She gets serious. Turns him and pushes him towards the door. "Think I saw that repo pest nosing around yesterday."

"I see him I'll repo his face. Gotta run. Luv ya," pulling her in for one last taste of her sweet lips before letting her go.

"Luv ya," patting his ass as he opens the back porch door and steps out into the box-lined back entryway.

Sage follows him out into the porch. Closes and locks the back door behind him. She peeks out the back door window curtain, watches him climb into his beat-up Olds Cutlass. It growls to life, backs out the curved gravel driveway and then disappears as it roars down the street headed for downtown and US HWY 75 south.

JOHNNY WAKES

3

Ariadne has a Kieth Richards look going with her dark wind-tangled hair, her Raybans, and her gaunt face. Her lanky figure is squeezed into tight black low-rise jeans, a hot pink tank, and, for a touch of class, a pearl necklace droops down between her almost nonexistent breasts. She's driving her convertible with the top down in the heat, cruising at full speed down a lonely two-lane blacktop headed toward Breckenridge, Minnesota.

Johnny Wonder slumps shotgun, clad in frayed Levis that are spotted with dark stains all up and down his legs. The stains may or may not be wood stain spills, since he enjoys making things out of wood. His long sleeve denim shirt is likewise stained. It hangs open down mid-chest showing-off a steampunk-ish vacuum tube necklace - his most prized possession. His sweaty flesh glistens in the bright sunshine, collecting the wheat-straw dust that seems to be floating in the air. He's just coming out of a stupor.

Ariadne, having just played text-tag, stuffs her phone back

into her ass pocket.

"Hey hotshot," playfully backslapping Johnny's shoulder. "You awake?"

Johnny rubs his eyes and looks around at the passing countryside; flat farmland far as the eye can see. Distant farm groves float like islands in the waving wheat. It's harvest time. Alongside the highway a combine grinds and mulches swathed rows of wheat loud as God. It spews out straw and chaff from its ass-end, filling the air with golden dust. Seeing it again brings back memories of when he was a boy helping his dad farm... and the painful crush he had on his cousin Doreen.

They come to a reflective green highway sign. Ariadne eases off the gas.

BRECKENRIDGE 8

Johnny does a double take. The name of his home town has been painted over in spray paint with a new name in large lurid red shaky letters:

NEW MANCHURIA

Seeing it, Johnny recalls the whole reason they're on the road - the Chinese Occupation. Johnny and Ariadne fled Hollywood because the Chinese Censorship Board forcibly cancelled his hit reality TV show America's Next Great Psycho - claiming there are no psychos in the new Chinese America. He begged to differ, taking his show on the road, into the American hinterland to find the last true Americans - psychos be damned. But now, it looks like there's no escaping the Red Virus.

"What the fuck is that shit?" Johnny says.

"Dorothy, we're not in Minnesota any more," looking over at him with concern. "Hun, you feeling okay?"

"Think I'm going to be sick."

"Not in this car you're not," slowing and studying him. He's pallid. Glaze eyed. "Hold on. I'll pull over."

She stops the car along the wide gravel shoulder. Johnny opens his door, leans out and dry heaves. He's eaten practically nothing the last twenty-four hours. Gets out. Tries to walk. The world spins. He falls against the hood of the car. He feels a painful bump on the back of his head.

Where'd that come from?

Ariadne rushes out and helps him. He tries to forget the Chinese and focus on something good. Like his memories of Doreen - how good she made him feel when they were together. Helps clear his mind and chase away the willies. If only he can cling to her image. He's got to get into town. Visit their old haunts. Uncover more memories of her. But he can't do that with Ariadne leading him on a leash.

She takes his hand, rubs it, pulls him up and hugs him.

"You have that far-away look," whispering in his ear. "What are you feeling?"

He pulls out of her embrace.

"Ariadne, I'm afraid this is the end of the road. I have to go on without you. I just need some time alone."

She slaps him hard, almost knocking him back onto the car.

"Sorry, sweetie. That was to wake you up. Alone out here the Chinese will crucify you... for what you did back in Hollywood." She tries to retake his hand but he steps around front of the car. She lets him go, pleading soft and tender, "Who has always bailed you out? Me. Your faithful agent."

He walks away from her, around to the other side of the car and impulsively jumps into the driver's seat, guns the engine, and shouts, "I appreciate all that but this is about my own personal past and I can't have you messing with my memories."

"It's about another woman, isn't it? Some lost love," grabbing the passenger door handle.

He shifts into drive and shoots ahead some twenty feet leaving her stumbling in the gravel.

"What are you going to do," shouting as she jogs up to the car. "Strand me out here in the sticks? Leave me to the coyotes and God knows what else?"

BLUE LETTER BIBLE

4

Snakes has driven out ten miles east of town. He does a u-turn on the two-lane blacktop, pulls over on the shoulder, and waits. He's still basking in the afterglow of sex with Sage. She has a goooood body and knows how to use it. Gives him a hardon just thinking about it. He's got a good thing going and doesn't want it fucked up by any extenuating circumstances. So maybe delaying delivery of the package a few hours would be to his advantage. Give him time to prep said package. Take out a little insurance against the possibility of things going sour.

He puts a Prince CD in the under-dash-mounted player and cranks it. Time to get funky. He opens the glove box and takes out the antique Colt .45 revolver Sage gave him on their one year anniversary (was her great grandfather's). It's got custom purple heart grips (purple is Snake's power color) with a coiled snake wood burned into one and his initials into the other. He spins its cylinder and sees a big fat round resting in each chamber. He sets the gun down on the seat beside him.

Reaching back into the glove box, he pulls out a black leather Bible. It's a special blue letter translation printed and distributed exclusively by the BROFOs - purported to be 98.4% pure word of God. Snakes turns to the story of the prodigal son in the Book of Luke:

It is right that we should party and rejoice: for thy brother was dead and is alive; was lost, and is found.

He reaches down and unsheathes a razor-sharp buck knife from his right boot. He uses the knife to scrape the blue words off the Bible's page, forms them into a neat line, leans forward with one nostril pinched and snorts the fine blue dust. His head bolts back like it's been hit by a shotgun blast.

"Yeah! Yeah! Fuck yeah! Praise Jesus."

He closes the Bible and sets it on the dash. Reaches back into the glove box and pulls out a pair of binoculars. Peers through them at the road up ahead. Sees a car sitting alongside the road a couple miles up. Time to get into character. Puts the binos back, gets out, opens the trunk. Takes out an old school cop car cherry (something Lt. Drebin might use), gets it flashing and puts it on the roof of the car. Speeds off towards the car up ahead.

ESCAPE FROM the CHINESE

5

Johnny and Ariadne see a car coming from the east. It's still a couple miles away but its flashing purple light casts a hushing spell.

"What the hell is that," Johnny says, head turned way around.

"Looks like a Chinese patrol car," clutching the door handle, panting. "Don't stare at it. They use purple lights for hypnotic effect."

"Gotta be on their way to some emergency in town, right?"

"Johnny, they're after you… and me. We should leave, now."

Johnny guns the engine and the car lurches from her grasp. He stops some ten feet ahead.

"Not so fast. Like I said, I'm going on alone. You're only eight miles from town. Go to Eleanor's Beauty Salon. She's a good old-fashioned woman. Take good care of you."

He shoots a glance down the road behind them. The flashing purple light is growing bigger by the second.

"Johnny we're more than just a team. I love you and I don't

want anything to happen to you. You leave me, they'll get me, and then they'll get you and send you back to Faye Qing."

Johnny flashes on what happened a week ago back in Hollywood. He was closing in on a psycho during the latest episode of America's Next Great Psycho. When, out of the blue, this dragon lady, Faye Qing, Head of the Chinese-American Censorship Board, a boat-load of censorship cops in her wake, slapped an injunction on him. Told him if he didn't comply he'd be spending the rest of his life in a Manchurian shoe factory. He and Ariadne fled, taking the show on the road, becoming fugitives.

They see the patrol car is now just a mile back and closing fast.

Ariadne rushes up to the car and dives into the passenger seat. She grabs Johnny's thigh and pulls herself in as he peels out onto the highway.

"Floor it, sweetie. Loose that bastard."

Johnny burns rubber, speeding off towards town.

"This conversation ain't over. Soon as we ditch the cops, you're out."

Johnny sees a gravel side road coming up and impulsively turns onto it. The chase car follows, closing. Johnny pours on the gas and raises a towering cloud of gravel dust, engulfing the cop car.

A mile up the road Johnny hits a stretch of loose gravel. His car fish-tails. He looses control and veers off the road, plowing into a dense patch of bushes behind a low-sitting billboard. The car crashes into one of the sign's telephone pole-sized supports. Not seat-belted, both Johnny and Ariadne are thrown from the car. Ariadne lands in the deep prairie grass and suffers only a few scrapes and bruises. Johnny, not so lucky, hits his head on the back of the billboard and blacks out.

DREAM of BULLHEAD

6

Zedung, D.C. - lately re-christened capitol of the Peoples United States of Chinese America. A D.C. Street. A news stand. The front page of the Wall Street Journal shows a photo of a high powered businessman along with the story of how he made his fortune off the busted backs of common people like you and me.

This CEO makes 500 million dollars.

A nerdy Asian man in a cheap suit reaches down and grabs the paper, reads it. Behind him the P.U.S.C.A. flag (red and gold stripes with fifty gold stars swimming in a field of red) flutters from a pole outside the former FBI Building.

But to Frankie Karpis,

looking up from the paper with fury in his eyes,

he's nothing but Capi trash.

In a whirlwind, Karpis scurrys into the former FBI Building (lately recommissioned as headquarters of the Peoples Resource Reclamation Bureau), down a polished hallway, into the mens room, and into a stall. He lifts the toilet seat and plunges head-first into the recently used commode.

Because his secret identity is...

On the banks of the filthy Potomac River, the monuments rise in the background. A dark quasi-human figure clad in scaly tights shoots out from the murky water. Fins flare from its arms and back. Gills dripping with slime pulsate all along its neck. Its head is that of a monstrous angry catfish.

Bullhead!

Bullhead has surfaced in Crystal City. He enters a glittering glass office tower. Moments later glass explodes from an upper-story window. Down swoops our hero burdened with two bulky objects, one in each fin. He dives back into the Potomac.

In the blink of a fisheye he's back at P.R.R.B., meandering through a sea of cubicles to the office of Special Agent Tiffany Smart - a foxy young blonde fiercely devoted to enforcing the Chinese Takeover. But sometimes she gets in a little over her head. That's when Bullhead lends a fin. He drops the burden he's carried back from Crystal City; two objects thudding heavily upon Agent Smart's desk - a sachet full of large unmarked bills, and the WSJ cover-story CEO's severed head.

Agent Smart gasps, then smiles, "These capitalist pigs never stand a chance against you, do they, Bullhead?"

"So sorry, ma-am," blood dripping from his razor-sharp fins. "There was boardroom full of swine against just humble Bullhead."

He flashes back to Crystal City, bursting into a luxurious high-rise boardroom looking out over D.C., his fins flared at the ready. A table-full of mobster execs draw machine pistols and open fire in a spray of bullets. The rounds bounce off Bullhead's Kevlar scales. In a flurry of fins their severed heads fall and roll onto the shiny rosewood board table.

Bullhead waddles through the pool of blood to an inner office. He busts the door in with a flick of his powerful tail, catching the fat cigar-puffing CEO in the act of shredding documents.

"What the hell," the CEO shouts. "Beat it, you sewage-sucking bottom feeder."

Bullhead walks over and flops down on the CEO's ebony desk.

"You're the stinky one. Stop shredding. You need to sign all of your holdings over to the Peoples United States."

"Eat my lead, fish lips," pulling out a machine pistol. He fires in vain while taking a fin to the neck.

The flashback dissolves as cubicle drone Frankie Karpis bashfully nudges up to Agent Smart (only she knows his secret super hero identity).

"Hardcore capitalist foreclosure deniers will never surrender their wealth alive," he says, recalling the time in a Georgetown yuppie watering hole when he carpeted the beer-stained floor with filleted bodies of a dozen young MBAs.

Karpis takes Smart in his arms and awkwardly kisses her.

"Then what?" she says. "Once the Capitalist menace has been vanquished?"

"And the streets are safe for Communism? Then we can swim off to that lake up in the north country you've always been dreaming of… and spawn."

"I want a whole school of little Commies," she giggles.

"No reason why we can't get started now," taking her hand.

They leave the P.R.R.B. And cross the street to a noodle house.

If you deny the Chinese Takeover, then you'll be sushi to Frankie Karpis on…

Karpis, walking towards a restroom, stops, slowly turns, and gazes nerdishly into space.

BULLHEAD.

Every weeknight at eight-thirty.
Karpis puts his hands together and bows.
Fade to black.

JEALOUS of KARPIS

7

Johnny is sprawled out on the grass in the three-foot-high space beneath the billboard. His legs are sticking out behind the sign while his head and torso lay sprawled out in front, eyes to the sky. He groans, semi-conscious.

Laying in the tall grass next to the billboard, Ariadne sits up, checks herself over - just a few bruises and scrapes, little shaken. She groans and gets up and staggers around the car. It's crunched up against one of the heavy support poles. She sees Johnny, hurries around front and squats down to see if he's alright.

"Oh, Johnny. Oh, Johnny. Talk to me."

"Ohhh," holding his head, the world slowly coming back into focus. "Ohh, Tara."

"You got a nasty bump," feeling his forehead. "Don't try to move."

"I've lost her," sobbing, he reaches for Ariadne and lets his head fall into her lap.

"Shh, shh, big boys don't cry... . Want to tell me what's going on?"

Johnny lifts his head and wipes his eyes with her tank and then lets it fall back down in her lap, hugging her slender hips.

"Don't know if it was a vision, a dream, precognition, or what.... I just saw a, a, a trailer for a new Chinese TV show... and, and those fuckers they're airing their goddamned show in *my* fucking slot. MY FUCKING SLOT. Fuckers. I need a cigarette. Got one?"

"Gave them to you, silly," reaches in his shirt pocket and pulls out a pack of Marlboros. She sticks one between his quivering lips, reaches deep into his pants pocket, takes out his Zippo, lights the cig, reaches back into his pants and replaces the lighter. "I can see that would be a problem, but nothing to cry over."

"That ain't the kicker," taking a long drag on the cigarette. He takes it from his lips and blows out a column of smoke, squeezes his eyes tight to fight back more tears and shouts, "They got that fucking Frankie Karpis playing the lead."

"That little ass-wipe who stole Tara from you?" She reaches into his shirt and caresses his chest, feels his thumping heart.

"She's in the show," chain puffing. "His love interest. FUCK!"

"Sweetie, let her go. Let's go into town. I'll help you look up Doreen. You'll feel better and you'll forget all about Tara."

"That's the fucking problem. Tara is Doreen. They could be the same girl for all I know - Doreen all over again, ten years older... and she's in love with this, this..." Looking up past Ariadne he sees the face of the billboard looming over them. It advertises a local restaurant, *The Old Mill*. It's a remodeled historic flour mill along the bank of the Doran Slough just south of Breckenridge (again, the town name has been painted-over with *NEW MANCHURIA* in lurid red graffiti). The restaurant has a deck over-hanging the water. On it, a fisherman is pulling out a huge angry fighting bullhead. "...

This, this fucking fish. FUCK!"

"C'mon," lifting his head out of her lap and getting to her feet. She helps him stand. "Can you walk? Lets go into town. Maybe this is all just a bad dream."

"It ain't no dream," limping. It's fucking bullshit is what it is."

Checking him over, "Your eyes are all red and puffy. No way to triumphantly return to your hometown." Checking the grass, she finds her Raybans and puts them on his face. He continues to chain smoke. She takes the cig from him and sticks it between her own lips.

Ariadne helps Johnny make it through the shallow ditch and up onto the highway. Looking to the east, emerging from the shimmering heat waves, they see a car coming towards them. Towards New Manchuria.

"Hey," Ariadne says. "Maybe we can hitch a lift."

HITCHHIKERS

8

Johnny and Ariadne start walking along the gravel shoulder of US Highway 75 towards town. They turn and see the approaching car slow down as it draws near.

"Play it cool," Ariadne says. "We don't know who we can trust."

The car, just a couple hundred feet away, slows to a crawl and angles to the side of the road. Johnny gets a good look at the driver.

"Don't worry," Johnny says. "I remember this asshole. You're right. He can't be trusted."

It's Snakes in his beat-up Olds Cutlass. He pulls to a crunching stop along side them, windows all down because of the heat.

He leans over toward the passenger side, grinning shit-eatingly, "You two sorry-looking sons of bitches look like you could use a lift." Eying Johnny up and down, seeing his stained clothes, "Shit, man. That ain't blood is it?"

Ariadne leans in through the open passenger door window. "We've just been in a minor accident."

Johnny leans in beside Ariadne. "Nothing serious. Just a little shook-up. Preciate that lift, though."

"On our way to look up old friends," Ariadne says.

"Well, shit," Snakes says. "Hop on in."

Johnny opens the passenger door, lets Ariadne slide into the front seat, and gets in after her, slamming the door shut. Snakes shifts into drive and heads off towards town, taking it slow and easy. Introductions all around.

"What's that you got hanging on your neck, bud?" Snakes says, eyeing Johnny's unusual necklace.

"Vacuum tube from an old TV," holding it up for Snakes, turning the small glass tube so he can see the tiny intricate array of fine wire grids and metal plates enclosed within. "Kind of a keepsake from my dad. He was an inventor. Experimented with these things."

"Cool. He's into electronics and old school shit like that?"

"Was into it. Died a few months back."

"Sorry, man."

"Don't sweat it. He was a good man. Anyway, in his later years he experimented around with Quantum Mechanics as applied to everyday life."

"Now that's some shit way beyond me."

"Yeah, me too. But I've been reading up on it over the summer. Trying to carry-on dad's research. Think he was searching for a way out of the mess the world's in."

"No shit? Make any progress?"

"Johnny's shared some of it with me," Ariadne says. "Fascinating stuff. There may be hope for us yet."

"Oh yeah? Like what?"

"Check this out," Johnny says. "In the Quantum world you can be both dead and alive at the same time."

"Ha ha," Snakes smirks at him. "You think your old man may be still alive somewhere through some Quantum miracle?"

"Swear to God. I ain't ruling it out… . And also, things that only might have happened, but didn't happen, can cause an actual real thing to happen."

"Now I know you're fucking with me. You're talking fairy tales. You're still hung-up on your old man - looking for a way to bring him back." Snakes tells Ariadne, "Grab the Good Book," pointing to the Bible sitting on the dash in front of her. "Would ya, tits?"

"For one thing," frowning at him. "I don't appreciate the sexual slur. And secondly, a *please* would be nice."

"Pretty please, Ms Ariadne."

Sighing, she reaches and grabs the Bible, hands it to him, "Just Ariadne would be fine, thank you."

"*Thank you.* Know your way around the Bible, Ariadne?" hands it back to her.

"Like you wouldn't know," taking it.

"Flip to Matthew 8:28 and read it for me, if you wouldn't mind… do I need a *please* on that, too?"

Ariadne flips him the bird with her left hand while opening the Book on her lap with her right.

"Blue letters?" Johnny says, looking over at it.

"A special scratch-n-sniff version. Go ahead, read. Let's hear what it has to say."

Ariadne reads: *And when he came into the countryside he met two possessed by demons. And they screamed "Why do you torment us, Son of God?" And they beseeched him to cast them out into a heard of swine. And he said unto them, Go. And they went out into the herd of swine: and the whole herd ran violently down a steep path into a lake and perished in the waters.*

"That's good," Snakes says. "Johnny, those Quantum ideas of yours are like those demons. Reason the world today is so fucked-up. What it needs is a good ole baptism. Ariadne, would you, *please*, do something for me?"

"Within reason."

"Take one of those nice painted nails of yours and scratch-off a few of those Bible phrases."

"You're kidding," giving him a funny look. She shrugs and starts scratching the letters with her index finger, turning the words into a fine blue powder. "What, you snort your Bible?"

"Trust me, it's one hell of a rush. Go ahead. Take some into your fingernail and hold it up to your nose."

She follows his instructions, taking a cautious sniff, "Oooh, baby. Johnny, you've got to try this," scooping another fingernail-full of the dust and holding it out to him. He leans forward and takes a healthy snort.

"Damn," his head jolting back. He shakes it wildly and grabs the dash to stabilize himself. "That is one serious wake-up call."

Laughing wildly, pounding the steering wheel, "Welcome to the real world, homey."

"So, sweetie," wrapping her arm around Johnny's shoulders and smacking her lips on his cheek . "You feel better, now?"

"Oh, yeah."

Snakes turns off the highway onto a gravel road.

"Taking the dump road into town?" Johnny says.

"Yeah, the Chinese got a checkpoint set up on the main road just as you get to town. Figured we'd avoid all that and come in the back way."

"Good idea," Ariadne says. "Whew, what's that stink," pinching her nose.

"Eden Acres Hog Ranch. Couple miles over there," pointing toward a distant tree grove. "Knew a guy from around here who had a small herd of hogs. Jordy Rabnow. You ever know him, Johnny?"

Ariadne lays her hand on Johnny's knee and squeezes.

"Yeah," Johnny says. "I knew him. He still around?"

"Can't say. Haven't seen him all summer. Think maybe the

Chinese got him. He was a weird one."

"How come they haven't gotten you?" Ariadne says.

"I know how to lay low."

"Being a snake, you'd know how."

"Funny cunt ain'tcha? Anyway, got a safe house in town. Can take you there. Give you some chow. Show you how to move around town without drawing a lot of attention... without getting Shanghaied."

Ariadne squeezes Johnny's knee harder and gives him a subtle nod while Snakes is checking the roads for cop cars.

"Take us there," Johnny says.

NEW MANCHURIA

9

The unpaved dump road takes them along the east side of town. It's full of potholes and washboards - feels like a sledgehammer pounding the bottom of the car. About a mile up they pass a green road sign garnished with three grey quarter-sized bullet holes:

NEW MANCHURIA
POP. 1,978

Lucky if it's half that. On their left they pass Wally's Wrecking and Scrap Metal. Mountains of twisted and tangled rusty iron and acres of junked cars spread out like a welcome mat greeting the weary traveler to the fair town.

"That's where I scored my baby here," Snakes says, patting the dash. "My junior year. Hundred and fifty bucks. Wally wanted three and a half bills. Was a real junker. Towed it home. Worked on it all that winter. Got it going in time for prom. Scored my first piece of ass in the back seat there," hitching his thumb over his right shoulder.

"That's a little more info than we needed," Ariadne says, scrunching up her nose and coughing. "God, doesn't that awful stench ever leave?"

"Eden Acres again. Spuds Dobson must be out spreading honey. Every east breeze blankets the town with the fragrant smell of hog shit. 'That's the smell of money,' Ma Dobson tells everyone. I've shoveled my share. How I paid for the Cutlass. Even deflowered a sweet young thing, who shall remain nameless, in the boar pen at the ranch that same summer."

"Please," Ariadne says, swiftly raising her right hand to Snakes' throat and digging her nails into his flesh, leaning close and hissing. "Spare us the details."

"No problemo," Snakes chokes.

Ariadne releases her death grip and sits back to checkout the approaching town.

Snakes turns left on Wilkin Avenue, goes bumpity-bump, bumpity-bump over twin railroad tracks, drives by the lumber yard and cruises to a stop at the intersection of Main Street.

Looks like there's nothing new in town. Tired old brown brick buildings and small plate-glass-fronted shops, staring back with vacant looks, line the street on both sides in both directions. Looks like the town got tired of trying to keep up with the times and just threw in the towel. You'll never in a million years find a Starbucks here. You'll have to settle for the weapons-grade prairie coffee at Kate's Diner (a greasy spoon catering to farmers and locals who like to go in and shoot the shit about who's fucking who around town and who's got the biggest tractor). If you're unlucky enough to breakdown in New Manchuria, there's Andy's Auto Repair. Andy's an honest guy. But if your car needs parts you might have to shack-up for the night at the King's Trail Hotel. The decor hasn't been redone since Nixon bamboozled the nation with his Checkers Speech, but the vibrating beds are a kick.

Ice machine crapped out during the Murdoch family reunion back in oh-six, though. So you'll have to run down the block to Ray's Market. Ray closes at ten, so don't wait too late. Hotel don't get cable, got no wifi. So, if you're bored, forget the Empire Theatre (been closed and boarded-up since *Silence of the Lambs* back in '92), but there's the two-lane bowling alley and Earl's Corner Bar - which is nice and handy being just across Wilkin Avenue (the Old Mill is about a mile south of town if you're hankering for something a little more classy and don't mind the walk). Don't even have to worry about traffic. Just stagger back to your room after last call. And when your head's hurting next morning, North Star Drugs has a fully stocked line of hangover remedies you can pop right into your mouth and wash down with a glass of New Manchuria's finest tap water filtered straight from the rushing waters of the Doran Slough. And while you're at North Star, pick up the latest copy of *The High Plains Dealer*, the town's daily rag, and don't forget to get a scenic postcard to make all your friends back home envious.

Snakes doesn't have to wait for traffic. There's no one out and only a few cars parked in front of the newspaper building and the bar. He takes a right on Main. Slows for a stray dog that comes trotting out from between buildings, and then drives down a couple blocks and hangs another right onto Mendenhall Avenue, cruising the next two blocks slow. The neighborhood is ghostly quiet - small working class wood frame houses falling into serious disrepair. Johnny counts seven abandoned. A dog barks somewhere on the next block. Snakes drives all the way to the end of the street, past a DEAD END sign. Nothing beyond that but ripe fields of grain far as the eye can see, a golden harvest haze hangs in the air.

"There it is," Snakes says, an air of pride in his voice about the dump coming up on their right. The lawn is more dirt than grass. Judging by the proliferation of auto parts and rusty iron laying around, the place could serve as Wally's annex. "Homey, ain't it?"

A yellow dilapidated wood frame two story in bad need of paint.

"A regular dream house," Ariadne says. "You landscape it yourself or contract out?"

Snakes ignores the sarcasm and turns into the driveway, pulls up to a stop in front of a cluttered double garage.

"C'mon in," killing the engine. He grabs the Colt .45 from under the seat and stuffs it in his pants. "Just a little insurance policy," he says, answering their inquisitive stares. "Like me, you guys are probably starving."

SAFE HOUSE

10

Snakes leads Johnny and Ariadne in. There's a chopper parked in his living room. Engine parts are scattered in the kitchen. Tools outnumber kitchenware on the counters. Beer signs, Playboy pinups, and a crucifix adorn the walls. Needless to say, the place smells like a garage.

Johnny leans against a filthy tool chest next to the kitchen table. Snakes goes over to the cupboards above the cluttered counter, opens them, checks what he has to offer for food.

"Kind a odd," Snakes says. "You driving all this way and no luggage."

"We had to leave in a hurry," Ariadne says, walking over to the sink. It's filled with day-old dishes bathing in cold greasy water. "Chased out of Hollywood by the censorship police."

"Let me guess," Snakes turns to Johnny, taking a closer look at the dark purple stains splattered all up and down his jeans. "Dress code violation.... One of those supermarket tabloids they got down at Ray's says you're into woodworking. When it came to wood, Jordy Rabnow was an artist. He was around… maybe he could give you a few pointers."

Ariadne walks over to Johnny, takes his hand, gives Snakes a dirty look. "Johnny's got more important things on his mind."

"And like, I'm supposed to believe those are woodworking stains," turning back to the cupboard and pulling out a can of beans.

"You should see the other guy," Johnny says, glaring at Snakes. "Cut the guilt trip. You've seen my show. You know what happens in it. Like Ariadne said, we were chased out mid-production. Had no time to change."

"Guess I forgot about your show," fishing for a can opener in a drawer. "Got some spare duds upstairs. Can help yourself."

"That would be much appreciated."

"You passed the stairs on the way in."

"Back in a few," Johnny says, walking out into the living room.

Snakes shoots a glance at Ariadne whose checking her nails. "Mind helping me rustle up some grub while he's up there getting decent?"

"This is beyond my help but why not," pulling herself over to the counter.

Upstairs in one of the bedrooms Johnny finds a sartorial nightmare of Goodwill clothes in garbage bags. In another, hanging in a closet, he finds some duds slightly higher up on the ladder of cool. Ten minutes later he comes strutting back into the kitchen in a pair of scuffed black leather pants and a blue *Old Mill* t-shirt. It sports a picture of the historic building with *Spirits and Fine Dining* tastefully scripted below. He pulls out a chair from the table next to the tool chest. It feels good to sit. On the table, Snakes and Ariadne have spread out a smorgasbord of opened cans of veggies, fruit, beans, spaghettis, minnie weinies, and a six pack of Hamms beer. Everyone digs in.

Snakes feints a punch to Johnny's face, "Took my best shit, fucker."

Not flinching, "Gotta look like a rockstar even in a shit hole like this."

"Get a lot of pussy out there in movie land?"

"Be sensitive. Johnny's going through a rough time."

"Fraid that's true," Johnny says, grabbing a can of Hamms, popping it, and taking a gulp. God, that hits the spot. "First the Chinese cancel my show. Then some slimy Chinaman steals my girl."

"So what's the problem, tough guy? Kick his ass. Take her back. Shit, I'll even fuckup this bastard for ya."

"Problem is, she's back there and I'm stuck out here in Shitsville. Should have never ran. FUCK," pounding the table, rattling the plates and cans. "Why couldn't I've just stayed?"

"You weren't in love," Ariadne says, sitting in the chair next to him, rubbing his thigh. "That's why. You were only obsessed."

Snakes has pulled up a chair on the other side of Ariadne. "You're starting to sound a lot like Rabnow. All obsessed-up and no social skills."

Johnny forks a minnie weinie and flicks it at snakes. "Will you shut up about that loser."

"Whoa, didn't mean to push your hot button, sport. Seriously, I really do want to help. So, who's this Tara?"

The CABINET

11

Johnny flashes on when he hooked Tara:

We met at the commissary one day. Between takes I liked to unwind by browsing through Woodworking Enthusiast Magazine. Tara just happened to be walking by my table. A picture of one of the featured pieces caught her eye.

"Oh-my-god," Tara said. "What is that?"

She stopped, ice coffee in hand, and leaned in for a close look. Her fresh scent and body heat got me all juiced with desire. Turned toward her, smiling, and slid the mag over so she could take a closer look. She took my breath away, her hair - as blonde as sunshine, and her eyes sparkling like sky-blue waters. She slid a slender finger onto the pic and purred seductively, "I'd do just about anything to have that cabinet. Perfect for my boudoir."

The piece was this curvy tall slender curio cabinet looking like something straight out of Dr. Seus. I knew right then that Tara owned me.

"Sorry for interrupting your lunch," Tara said. "Mr. Wonder... ."

"Oh, Johnny, please."

"Thanks. Johnny, that cabinet is one of the most gorgeous things ever."

"Certainly does have a charm about it. But, unfortunately, I don't think it's for sale. It's one of a kind."

"Ohhh," she rubbed a fist into her left eye and pouted.

"Bet I could make one just like it for you."

BACK in BUSINESS

12

"That cabinet was my ploy for meeting Tara every day," Johnny says, taking a drink of beer. "It's construction was a collaboration. I'd give her progress reports. Show her pics. Through it we got close."

"Pshaw," Ariadne says, flicking her hand in the air. "She's just a bimbo who used you. Get over it."

"Don't you ever say that again," pointing a finger in her face.

"Okay, okay, chill."

Johnny sits back and lets out a deep breath. "She reminds me of Doreen."

"Doreen Norde?" Snakes says, spooning beans, corn, peas, and weenies onto his plate. "C'mon, you two, dig in. Doreen Norde who disappeared way back when?"

"Go ahead, Ariadne. I ain't hungry... yeah, way back when I lived here. She was my first love."

"First obsession," Ariadne says, filling her plate with corn and peas.

"Fuck you."

"Don't you see," Snakes says, his mouth seeping at the corners with food. "This is perfect. While in town, you can investigate her disappearance for… ."

Ariadne, chewing slowly and thoroughly, nods and gives Snakes a thumbs-up, "For America's Next Great Psycho."

"Right," Snakes continues, washing his food down with a gulp of Hamms and then belching. "You solve a long standing mystery, put the killer on the show, win back the slut, and ride off into the sunset. Perfect Hollywood love story."

"Good idea but easier said than done," Johnny says, finishing his first beer. He grabs another, pops it, takes a slurp, and leans back at an angle with his right arm draped over the old oak chair's backrest. He's liking the way the beer is starting to take the edge off his Bullhead-induced anxiety. "Let me tell you why. No crew. No camera. And this censorship bitch Faye Qing is on my ass."

Johnny is interrupted by the whizzing sound of a small engine they hear approaching the back of the house. He's all paranoid. Has he been discovered? Informed upon? He looks at Snakes. But Snakes is brewing up an anger-storm - thunder cloud eyebrows, lower lip jutting out, kicks back his chair, goes over and glances out the kitchen window.

The sound of the engine suddenly dies right out back. The back door creaks and Richie Hardly, Snakes' nerdy younger brother, steps softly into the kitchen, guilt written all over his face.

"Took the minibike without asking again, didn'tcha?" Snakes says, stomping over to him.

"You weren't around. I needed to see Armada."

"You wanna fuck Mongo McPhearson's dike daughter get your own wheels."

Snakes pulls his motorcycle-drive-chain-belt from his khaki pants and bitch whips Richie across the shoulders. Richie withers to the floor in pain.

"You're a real asshole," Ariadne shouts at Snakes, rushing to help Richie up and into a chair, gets him a beer, introduces herself and Johnny and fills him in on their problem.

"I know where you can get a camera," Richie says, the pain in his shoulder easing up a little. "Mongo saved all the outdated photo class stuff that the school was throwing out. He's got a regular vintage media lab in his basement."

"And it still works?" Johnny says, his eyes bulging. "Think he'll let us use it?"

"I don't see why not," blushing… "I've been using it to film Armada's workouts."

"Fucking pervert," Snakes says, threading his belt back into its belt loops.

Ariadne gets up and hugs Johnny. "Darling, we're back in business," kissing his cheek.

"Well fuck, this is the break you need," Snakes says. "I say we hop on our horses and pay old Mongo a call."

"My sentiments exactly," Johnny says, finishing his second beer.

The ZAPRUDER SPECIAL

13

Snakes leads the way to the garage out behind the safe house. Inside, under tarps are three beautifully restored vintage Arctic Cat minibikes (like the one sitting outside that Richie borrowed, but each a different model: a Screamer, a Whisker, a Prowler, and a Climber).

"Grab a bike and hop on," Snakes says, giving a brief operating tutorial. "You put so much as a scratch on one of these babies, your ass is grass."

They kick-start their machines and ride through the back alleys of New Manchuria. While crossing Wilkin Avenue they spot a Chinese cop car parked outside the library. But manage to make it the seven blocks to Mongo McPhearson's house undetected.

Entering the alley leading up to the McPhearson place, Snakes lets up on his throttle . They all follow his lead - their engines slowing to soft purrs. The leafy trees shelter them from the unrelenting sun. All is deathly quiet. They kill their engines and pull off the gravel onto a weedy patch of grass next to Mongo's Chrysler New Yorker beached under an ancient elm.

Mongo is a retired school teacher who taught Mass Media class and had a reputation for being a real hard-ass. He is still a large and lumbering, intimidating old codger - hence the nickname. He lives with his granddaughter, Armada, in an old Victorian house along the banks of the slough on the far west side of town.

Armada, having inherited her amazonian physique from Mongo, is into bodybuilding. She hopes to one day work as a stunt woman in the movies. Believing that it will lead to her being *discovered*, she lets Richie film her workouts and post them online.

"Back in the day," Snakes says. "Couldn't go into this old fart's class without a good shot of courage." pulling a fifth of Southern Comfort out of his inner jacket pocket. Takes a swig, and passes it around.

"Move and you're worm fodder," a scratchy voice, tremulous with phlegm, says. All heads (Johnny with the bottle to his lips) turn toward the old elm. A bulky bow-legged old man in a brown and yellow plaid bathrobe and nursing-home-slippers steps out from behind the tree. Long strands of wispy white hair halo his bald head. Thick speckle-lensed glasses rest precariously on the bulb of his pocked nose. He holds a double barreled shotgun leveled at Johnny. A basket of cucumbers and tomatoes hangs in the crook of one elbow.

Johnny starts to freak, the sight of a shotgun pointed at him triggering a traumatic episode from his boyhood.

"Now just take it cool, Mr. McPhearson," Snakes says, pulling the .45 out of his pants and forcing a Mexican standoff. "We're all friends here."

"That's right, sir," Richie says, hands in the air. "It's just me, Richie Hardly, my brother, Snakes, and two friends."

"What do you want?" lowering the gun just a little (only

because it's starting to get heavy).

"Sir, I don't know if you remember me. I'm Johnny Wonder. Had you for photography class a few years back."

Stepping closer, "Your face does look familiar, though I don't recall the name."

"Yes, it's nice to see you again. Your class inspired me to get into movie making. I've been in Hollywood. This here," gesturing toward Ariadne at his side. "Is my agent, Ariadne... . Well, to cut to the chase, we've come back to town to shoot a TV show on the disappearance of Doreen Norde."

"Yes, terrible tragedy. Lovely girl," lowering the gun butt to the dirt and leaning on the barrel cane-like.

"Great, great, you remember her. Well, we've got a bit of a production problem. See, the Chinese have confiscated all our filming equipment. But, Richie here tells me you still have some old movie cameras saved from your class."

"Yeah, yeah, the good old American made stuff. Can't find quality equipment like that any more. Got a mint condition Bell & Howell. You're welcome to it. Happy to see it put to use again. Hell, where's my manners, come on in," picking up the gun by its barrel and waving his arm. He turns toward the house's back door which is about a hundred feet up through the grassy yard. "Just about ready to cook up some chow. I'll feed you and then show you the equipment."

Inside the house Armada, seductively sporting tight cami yoga pants and a *property of U of M Athletic Dept.* tee cut at the gut showing off her chiseled abs, a backwards turned ball cap, and flip-flops, is mixing up a power shake. There's a mess of hash browns, eggs and bacon frying on the stove - more than enough for everyone. Despite Snakes' canned delicacies back at the Safe-house, they sit down to a good old fashioned brunch (even Johnny can't resist the aroma of down-home cooked food) while bitching about the Chinese and reminiscing about Mongo's glory days of oppressing his students.

Afterwards, they leave the dirty dishes for later (Mongo being anxious to show-off his treasures) and descend down into the basement.

It's like entering a time capsule. The basement's main room is carpeted and wood-paneled, furnished with a couch, a couple vintage 60's easy chairs, and a huge dinosaur vacuum tube-powered TV set (Johnny's heart melts upon seeing it). Obviously, in the remote past the room had served as a family room. Now, it seems more like a storage area; antique and out-of-date stuff like typewriters, toys from the 60's and 70's, a cassette player with a box of cassette tapes, boxes of old back issues to Time and Life magazine, and piles of vintage clothing. On one table sits a bulky brushed-steel 8mm movie projector, its lens pointed at a patch of white plastered wall on the opposite side of the room.

"So this must have been your viewing room back in the day," Johnny says, kneeling down to the projector and fingering it's switches with a kind of religious reverence. The machine's not plugged in. Nothing happens.

"Every Saturday night," Mongo says. "That cabinet behind you there, has all the reels of film I shot over the years; family vacations, holidays, school events, the county fair, trips to the lakes... . Come on," waving his arm and turning toward a dark doorway. "I'll show you the photo lab."

He leads the way, flipping a light switch, revealing a tidy laundry room with a closed door to the left. He opens it, flips on the lights, lets everyone crowd in, and starts pointing out various devices that sit on workbenches around the small room - explaining a little about each object as if he's giving a school tour, "That's the enlarger, over there we have the splicer, that cabinet there is for supplies and, behind that door with the red light is the dark room."

Johnny's eyes lock onto a crescent-shaped black leather case with a chrome latch and matching chrome trim. Embossed in silver letters along the front is the brand name, *Bell & Howell*, followed by an insignia proclaiming, *Director Series / Electric Eye*.

"May I, sir?" Johnny's hands reaching for the case.

"Be my guest, young man," Mongo says, chuckling over Johnny's excitement. "But be gentle. She's over sixty years old."

Fingers trembling, Johnny flips up the silver clasp and tilts open the lid. His jaw drops seeing the pristine condition of this rare jewel. "An actual *Zapruder Special Zoomatic AR414!*"

"Yes, my boy. It's a legend. Same make and model that caught JFK in his moment of demise."

Shaking his head in disbelief, Johnny reaches in and carefully pulls out the movie camera. It's black brushed steel with pebbled black cowhide panels on each side and fronted with a band of brushed aluminum. It feels solid and heavy in his hands, about the size of a small machine pistol (without the grip and trigger), its blunt offset lens standing in place of a barrel. Holding it gives Johnny a sense of power.

"Well then," Ariadne says. "It only seems fitting that we use such an iconic camera to capture America's Next Great Psycho."

"Yes… yeah… yeaaaah," looking through the *Zapruder Special's* view finder, Johnny pans the room. "It'll give us that raw feel, that *Blair Witchy* feel. How much film ya got, Mr. McPhearson?"

"Enough for ten feature films over in yon fridge," Armada says. "Gramps can even develop it in the dark room."

"Fantastic! It's okay for us to use it, then?"

"Sure, you betcha. Long as you treat it like a baby" Mongo says. "Happy to see it get some use again. Just what kind of project you people got going, anyway? You mentioned something about a TV show."

"Mongo... er, Mr. McPhearson," Ariadne says, putting her hand on the venerable old teacher's shoulder like he's the newest addition to their production crew. "Johnny here is the star of a sort of vigilante TV show that hunts down psycho killers who have slipped through the justice system. However, due to the extreme style of vengeance he brings to these maniacs, the censors have cancelled his show and confiscated all his equipment - more or less placing a bounty on his own head. This is why he needs to borrow your camera - so he can solve the Doreen Norde case and execute extreme prejudice on her abductor."

"We suspect she was brutally murdered, "Johnny adds. "And her killer is living right here among us."

"Man," Snakes says, pounding his fist into his hand. "We're gonna track down this scum bag and give him what he deserves - slow, painful justice."

"If you can achieve that," Mongo says, his voice shaky with anger. "It would really lift the spirits of this God forsaken community. I'm behind you all the way. What is your first course of action?"

"Thank you, sir," Johnny says, hugging the camera like it's his baby. "What we need now is a production meeting. Plan out our shooting."

"Yes," Ariadne says. "Without a script we'll be more or less winging it."

"Let's blow this cave," Armada says, heading toward the door. "Fucking gorgeous outside. We'll get some beverages and hit the back deck."

"Love the way you think," Richie says, following her, the others close behind.

PRODUCTION MEETING

14

"Alrighty then," Johnny says, stepping out onto the bright sunlit deck, grinning ear-to-ear, Ariadne at his side. Everyone else has already eased themselves into comfy patio chairs clustered around a table. Mongo has generously supplied iced tea and Schmidt beer.

"So what's the plan, boss," Snakes says, reaching into a cooler, pulling out a can of Schmidt, and tossing it to him.

"Sounds like we're ready to get down to it," Johnny says, catching the beer one-handed, water droplets spraying. He pops it and takes a swig. "Richie, sounds like you're well acquainted with the Zapruder. You're my camera man."

"Already got it locked and loaded and ready for game," patting the movie camera sitting on the table in front of him.

"And I can do sound," Armada says, sitting beside Richie, a mic-ed-up portable Craig reel-to-reel recorder sitting on the table in front of her.

"Fucking right on. Let's get that sucker rolling. Our production meeting'll be a good lead-in for the show.

Cool," Richie and Armada say in unison, grabbing their

equipment and getting up. They step back to the south side of the deck so the sun is over their shoulders. Richie has everyone reposition themselves around the table with Johnny in the center, Ariadne and Snakes at his sides (Mongo complaining that his caveman-looks might break the lens, prefers to stay out of the picture, moving back into the shadows along side the house but close enough to offer constructive criticism to Richie).

"Ready? Roll em," Johnny says, smiling into the lens, he improvs an intro, adopting his down-home congenial yet authoritative screen voice. Richie presses the Zapruder's start button down to RUN and Armada presses PLAY and RECORD on her Craig, holding the microphone out towards Johnny.

"Howdy fans, welcome to a new edition of America's Next Great Psycho. This week we have what promises to be our most challenging and dangerous show to date. Not only are we on the trail of a potential pedophile and murderer, but we have to dodge the Chinese censorship cops to boot. I hope we catch this culprit. Hell, I hope we make it out of this hell hole alive. We're here on location in lovely New Manchuria, Minnesota… as media outlaws. Let me introduce the crew. On my right, my agent and provocateur, the lovely and perspicacious Ariadne. On my left, my big bold body guard, Snakes Hardly. Snakes, are you packing," both Johnny's gaze and Richie's lens turning towards Snakes.

"Hey, you fuck," Snakes shouts, sneering at the camera, opening his leather jacket, showing off the .45 stuck in his belt. He leans back, lifts up his left leg and bangs his motorcycle boot down on the table, shaking beer cans. He pulls a buck knife out of the boot and flashes it - sun rays sparkling off its razor-sharp blade. "We're comin' to get your ass," jabbing his finger into the lens. "Your ass is mine, perv."

"Easy, dude, easy," Johnny says, nervously smiling as he

turns back to the camera. "Don't want to scare off our perv before we bag him. On with the introductions. Behind the scenes, our director of photography is Snakes' younger brother, Richie Hardly. And, doing sound and hopefully a few death-defying stunts, the beautifully fit and chiseled Armada McPhearson. Turn the camera on Armada... there you go." Richie steps back and pans to his girlfriend. "Flex for the viewers, Armada..." She rolls a sleeve over her powerful shoulder and curls her arm, bicep popping, smiling proudly. "Wow! Have you ever seen biceps like that on a girl? I know I haven't. Snakes, if you need any help with the perp... whew. Sure is getting hot out here." Richie turns the camera back onto Johnny. "Okay, last but not least, former high school media studies teacher, our technical advisor, the one and only Mongo McPhearson." Richie does a quick hundred-and-eighty to Mongo who waves him off. He pans back to Johnny. "Now here's our plan. After a few establishing shots of the town, we'll go on location to the last known whereabouts of a tragic young girl, Doreen Norde, who disappeared at the young age of twelve... ," Johnny gets emotional, briefly tears-up, stumbles over words, and has to pause. Ariadne motions for Richie to CUT. She helps Johnny compose himself and, after a few minutes, they get the camera rolling again. "We"ll dig up clues," wiping his eyes. "Interview neighbors, relatives, take a peek inside the house she lived in, and pick up the trail of her abductor. We're gonna do this show gonzo-style. On the run. Raw and improve so that you... ," pointing at the camera. "The viewer, will be here with us, down-n-dirty, along for the ride," holds a long confident smile. "And, CUT," swiping his right hand across his throat. Johnny lets out a deep breath and switches back to his normal everyday voice. "How did it look, Richie?"

"You looked fabulous, Johnny. Light was good and I zoomed in on Snakes' gun and knife, and on your tears for emotional resonance."

"Great. Great work everybody. Let's take five, pack our gear and hit the streets while we still have light. We've got ourselves a show!"

The DORAN SLOUGH

15

The crew, sitting on Mongo's deck, continues to film Johnny and Ariadne as they establish the context for the show.

"Johnny," Ariadne says. "Can you give our viewers an idea of who Doreen was, what she was like? You were one of the last to see her the night she disappeared, right?"

"Th, that's absolutely right, Ariadne. And, as painful as those memories are, it's plumb necessary for you to have a vivid picture of that vivacious young girl...," pausing, he lowers his eyes in thought. "It was actually down along the slough... hell, let's everybody go down to the water." He turns to Ariadne, "I know you don't like water, but we need to get an establishing shot." Back to the others, "C'mon, everybody."

Johnny leads everyone down the deck steps and across two hundred feet of un-mowed back yard to the water's edge. The Doran Slough is about a hundred feet wide with swift current, lined on both sides by tall old oaks and elms. Mongo has a redwood dock that reaches twenty-five feet out over the muddy water. A rowboat with a horse-and-a-half motor is tied to the end. Johnny, Snakes, and Richie (camera rolling) and Armada (Craig recording) walk out onto the dock. Ariadne and Mongo stand safely on the bank and watch.

Looking up stream about a quarter mile through golden-green hazy humidity, they can see the iron trusses of the Wilkin Avenue bridge.

Johnny points up that way, "It was about half a mile up stream, past the bridge. You can't see it from here. It was just past that bend in the slough. I lived with my parents in a house on the far side. It was late at night, about this same time of year. I'd snuck out to launch my latest model rocket - was twelve at the time. Same age as Doreen. Ran into her by chance."

Johnny sinks his head into his hands, his shoulders shaking, visibly stirred.

"Oh, Johnny," Ariadne says. She covers her eyes so as not to look at the water and cautiously walks out to him the dock. Hugs him. She tenderly tells him, "Tell the viewers what you're experiencing. Give us the gritty details. Leave nothing out, no matter how trivial. It might be a clue .

Johnny composes himself and lifts his head, addressing the camera, "Yeah, sure… . It's as if it were yesterday. Like I said, It was the dead of night… ."

The NIGHT DOREEN DIED

16

Must have been twelve when I first got into serious rockets. Bottle rockets bought for the Fourth of July got me going. From there moved on up to solid fuel powered kits from Radio Shack. But they didn't give me the kick I needed. So I graduated to sugar rockets. Homemade jobs learnt from Youtube. It was one of my "sugar babies" that I launched one fateful summer night some ten years back.

All wass quiet except for the croaking of frogs along the slough, the chirping of crickets in the surrounding high grass, and the rumblings of a distant freight train on the other side of town.

I mentally counted down from ten.

"...two... ignition," pressing my thumb on the igniter button.

WOOSH

"Yes," pumping my fist.

My faithful companion, Shep, barked loud enough to send echoes across the water. I petted him and gently told him the

"Shhhh."

Shit that was loud, looking back behind me up at the dark house a hundred yards away. No lights went on. *Houston, we have a go. They're still asleep.*

"Holy crap." Gazing high up into the moonlit sky, my eyes following the pale ghost-like vapor trail that curly-cued up towards the stars.

"Wouldn't it be cool to be up there in it? In a real one?"

Jumping at the sound of the voice, I turned and saw Doreen Norde, the tomboyish daughter of the pastor at Church of the Open Wound - she and her dad live next house up. She slinked towards me like a lynx, coming up from the muddy river bank.

I tried to act cool. But couldn't hide the thrill of seeing the hottest girl in the eight grade alone with me in the dark, in the wild. Don't think I haven't noticed she's just coming into her womanly parts. If there was anyone I wouldn't mind being here on my secret mission, it would be Doreen. Her cutoffs hugged her slender hips and her peach-colored tank had GIRL POWER glittered across her blossoming chest.

"Doreen! What are you doing out here?" Shep, tail wagging, tramped up to greet her. She smiled, ruffled his ears, and came over to join me.

"Didn't mean to scare you," smiling into my face and then up at the rapidly shrinking rocket in the sky. "You make that yourself?"

"Yeah, it's my first successful launch. First few exploded on liftoff. When mom saw the burnt grass out back she threw a fit, 'One of these days that darn kid is going to get us all killed.' That's why I'm down here this late. What's your excuse? Why you out here?"

"Couldn't sleep. Too sweaty and sticky in my room. Came out to cool off," biting her lip and giving me a mischievous sideways look. "So, ah, I didn't know you were into this kinda thing. You must be really smart and talented, huh?"

"Oh, well," blushing. "Guess I'm sort of a science nerd. Like to build things and experiment around. Get it from my dad."

"Right. Can't wait to take his shop class next year."

"Wouldn't that be cool if we had it together," almost drooling.

"Totally. Well, tell me about that thing up there. How big is it?"

"That baby up there," pointing up at it. "I've dubbed the *Intrepid*. Made completely from scraps found at Walley's junk yard. Three feet long. Two inches in diameter. Aluminum bodied... "

As I expounded on the finer details of the *Intrepid*, Doreen gravitated closer, causing the little hairs on my arms prick up as they brushed her soft flesh. I contemplated slyly putting my arm around her shoulders as we both gazed skyward, marveling as the *Intrepid* spent its fuel. A discharge at the tip ejected its nosecone trailed by a parachute blossoming like a dusky white rose.

"This isn't just for fun, you know," I confessed, turning my face to her. She's just slightly taller than me but I don't mind.

"Oh? Is this something I should know about?" returning my look, her eyebrows arched. Head tilted.

"Oh, yeah. There's a passenger up there. My pet frog, Hoppy Von Braun."

"Hahaha," slapping my shoulder hard. "You nut."

"No, seriously. He's the first frog in space. You've just... witnessed... history."

"What's wrong?"

"Oh shit."

As Hoppy and the *Intrepid* began their smooth descent back to earth a slight air current started blowing them over toward the unfriendly airspace of old man Goodman's place just across the river.

"Shit. Shit. Shit. No, come back," waving wildly, I tried to magically draw it back home. Old man Goodman was the meanest, orneriest old bastard in town. He had a weedy, run-down place that no one ever visited. He protected his hoard of junk with a shotgun and a vicious pitbull named Jaws - no relation to the famous shark, at least none that anybody knew of.

"That sucks. Well, I guess we'll just have to classify this mission as lost in space," turning to head back up to the house.

"Like hell we will," grabbing the back of my T-shirt, yanking me to a halt and spinning me around by the shoulders, face-to-face, her candy-breath hot on my cheeks. "You worked your ass off building that sucker and we're sure as shit not letting Hoppy be dog food for Jaws."

"Yeah, right. You want us to swim across the muddy slough, creep over and trespass on Goodman's place, rescue the *Intrepid* and Hoppy without being shot or mangled, and make it back home in time for breakfast, which is about an hour away, without blowing our cover, risking my ass being mangled into hamburger by mom's hairbrush and grounded till the next lunar eclipse which is scheduled to happen some time in 2015?"

"Captain Kirk wouldn't pussy out."

"Oh, you play dirty."

"Besides, wanna know the real reason I was out here this late?" winking with that devilish grin of hers.

"Uh-huh, what?"

"I like to skinny dip," turning, she fast-as-lightnig pulled off her tank, tucked it into the back of her cutoffs, and sprinted screaming to the river, dove in, and breast stroked to the opposite bank.

Shep followed in after her.

My jaw dropped in awe, paralyzed in wonder. *Get out there, dumb shit.* Next thing I knew I was jumping in after them. I swam like an Olympian in hope of getting a peek at paradise but she was too fast. I had to settle for silver. By time I got to where they waited she'd already got her tank back on. But, of course, with the wet fabric and cool night air, I was amply rewarded for following her on this suicide mission. The tall reeds along the bank helped hide my embarrassing enthusiasm.

We plodded inland, smelling like landed catfish. A few feet up we came to a barbed wire fence, marking the beginning of old man Goodman's property. We ignored the faded NO TRESPASSING sign nailed to a rotted wooden fence post and ducked between the rusty wire strands.

"I hope your tetanus shot is up to date," I said, following her through.

"I'm good," stopping to hold open the gap. I crawled through and did the same for Shep. We clomped through the muck of Goodman's deserted pasture, all the way up to the edge of his yard, crouching low behind an old dying elm - the gathering morning mist heavy with skunk.

Shep started sniffing around the grass.

"Don't you go running off now, boy" patting his head. "We need you to protect us from Jaws."

The pale glow of the yard light made everything look a little creepy - like one of those old time black and white TV shows that came on dad's old set. Deep shadows, hiding who knows what horrors, grew out from beyond the circle of light.

"Spooky," Doreen whispered.

We did a quick eyeball check of the yard, looking for jaws. He could've been hiding anywhere in all the junk lying around.

"There," Doreen pointed at a white lump sleeping in the doorway of a small doghouse around the corner from the porch on the south side of the house. "If we're quiet, don't think he'll bother us."

"If we're lucky, the old man will be asleep, too. Don't see any lights on in the house," scanning the old run-down farmhouse with its blistered white paint and bare grey siding and dark sunk-in windows looking back like death itself. "You sure we should go through with this?" hoping she would come to her senses and back down. Even in the dim clammy air, I could see the goose flesh rising on our arms.

"We're not pussies," punching my chest, pursing her lips and giving me a hard look with her piercing brown eyes. "You're a scientist and this is an adventure. We're in this together and we don't back down. Got it?"

"Roger that," grinning wide-eyed at her moxie. "Well, where did she fricking come down?"

We scanned the weed-choked yard, looking for a ruffled parachute, praying it hadn't gotten hung up in one of the many tall trees circling the yard. Nothing. But, then, the horror of horrors caught my eyes.

"Shit, there she is," nudging Doreen with my elbow (it felt good to touch her bare skin with my bare skin. The thrill gave me courage.) and pointing at the house. The *Intrepid* was resting on the short roof above Goodman's porch. "Now what do we do? No trellis. No drain pipes to climb."

"No, but there is a window above it."

"Yeah, but... ."

"But, your ass, we're going to sneak past Jaws, silently creep into the house, go upstairs, climb out that window and, like special forces, rescue your poor adorable pet frog and salvage your fantastic rocket. You got a problem with that?"

"Pure suicide," shaking my head but smiling in wonder at the balls this girl was making me grow. If I was going to die, it might as well be with the hottest babe in Wilkin County.

Doreen smiled with just barely a hint of blush, gave my

shoulders a tight squeeze and pecked me on the cheek. Now I was the one blushing and flying so high nothing old man Goodman could do could ever phase me.

We dashed to the cover of a small rock pile, about a hundred feet from the house. And then, gave Shep stern orders to sit and not move until we called him. He was a good dog and followed our commands.

Doreen took the lead. Wary-eyed, we crouch-ran through the barnyard grass to a dirt path leading up to the wooden porch steps. The heavy inside door to the house stood wide open, leaving just the screen door to deal with. I reached to open it, but Doreen grabed my hand, stopping me.

"We can't let it squeak."

"How do you know these things?"

"I sneak out a lot all the time," slowly pulling my hand, and the door with it, open - just enough for her slender hand to reach in and unhook the rusty old spring. That done, we opened the door without so much as a squeak.

"This is it," gazing into each others eyes, knowing the gravity of the situation. "No turning back now." She took my hand and, my heart thumping wildly (it's the first time I'd ever held a girl's hand and the feeling is pure ecstasy), we stepped into the grungy porch. The floor was broken linoleum but that didn't bother this country boy's bare feet. Now that Doreen and I were practically boyfriend and girlfriend, I wanted to be macho, and took the lead.

We stepped up out of the porch and into the kitchen. It was dark and dirty and quiet inside. That is, except for the unnaturally loud ticking of the wall clock. We still had forty-five minutes before D-hour. The kitchen stunk like something old and unwashed and of nasty stewed cabbage.

"Yuk! Gives me the willies," squeezing her hand tighter. "But there's something strange and fascinating about all this. Let's look around a bit before heading upstairs."

"Yeah, it's safe. Goodman's probably sleeping upstairs."

A mishmash of nails, bolts, washers, small hand tools, and various odd gadgets cluttered the kitchen table - a farm kid's dream. Too bad the place was an ogre's den.

"Fuck... ," breathing the word as I stopped dead. "Sorry."

"Pfft. I drop the f-bomb all the time. What is it?"

"Is that what I think it is," pointing at a long dark metallic object leaning against the grimy wallpaper between the refrigerator and the doorway.

"It is," both of us cautiously approaching. A sliver of yard light gleamed off its barrel. Goodman's notorious shotgun.

It almost seemed alive. It definitely possessed a certain evil power. I stared at it, hypnotized by its murderous reputation. I watched my own hand as it slowly drew near it, touching its cold barrel with one finger, like it was something that might bite back. Swallowing hard, I wrapped my fist around it and pulled it up closer, still holding Doreen's hand. She watched me with wild eyes as I brought it up to my nose and sniffed its business end, inhaling the intoxicating, nostril-biting tang of burnt powder.

"Recently fired," I breathed.

"Fuck," she whispered, the word hot upon my cheek as she leaned into me to took a sniff for herself. The smell made her eyes roll up and a tiny spasm rippled under her skin. "Is the body of some poor kid buried out back under the chicken coup?"

In a flash, I reconsidered the necessity of retrieving the rocket, and the need to see how Hoppy had fared. But, despite the gruesome risk, I was with Doreen and I had to do the right thing. She was right, the integrity of scientific inquiry demanded that I continue on. I imagined myself going down in history as a martyr to science, my picture hanging in every middle school science classroom right next to those of Neil Armstrong and Thomas Edison.

"What's that?" we both whispered at once like guilty kids caught in a forbidden act, our heads turning to look at the door on the other side of the kitchen. It was open just a crack. Bug-eyed, we watched it move ever so slightly, going, "Creeeeak."

"Maybe just a draft," I said, putting the gun back down.

We tip-toed over and inched the door all the way open. Behind it, a dark and cluttered passageway led to what looked like a seldom used front door. On the right wooden stairs disappeared up into the gloom.

We stepped forward, stopped and cocked our ears toward the second floor.

I heard two things, the beating of my own heart, and the somewhat more distant sound of jagged snoring, like that of a buzz saw laboring through knotty wood.

"Old man Goodman," we both gasped.

No matter how much I hated it, I had to go up there. It was the only way to get on the roof and rescue Hoppy.

Being weary of creaky boards, I led the way up that staircase to hell, testing each step with a sensitive toe, stepping only along the more trustworthy sides, taking them slowly. Doreen followed, her hand gently on my back. Midway up, a bad board betrayed us. We froze, holding our breathes, ready for retreat.

The snoring stopped.

It seemed like an eternity passed.... .

A phlegmy cough.

The snoring started back up.

We resumed our slow cautious climb.

At the top we entered an open attic-like space. Bushel baskets filled with wheat seed sat along the stairwell on the left. Long leafy plants dangled from a rafter drying. A spool of twine. Gunny sacks. They all added to the suffocating atmosphere. I covered my nose, breathing through my mouth. An extremely large fly buzzed my cheek, zig-zagged off to a dreary window, and kami-kazied the pane. Unfortunately, the window we needed was in the room on the right, the one with all the snoring.

Goodman's bedroom. Its door stood wide open. Doreen and I exchanged tentative glances. She motioned with her head towards the evil lair. Sweat was beading on my face, arms, and hands. I squeezed her hand tighter. She was sweating just as bad as me. I licked my dry lips, swallowed hard and, side-by-side, we crept over to the edge of the doorway and peered inside. It was gloomy as hell and hard to see. Slowly things began to take shape.

I'd never been this close to the old man. He was lying on his back in grubby long johns on a small cot. A rat's nest of white hair encircled his bony head. His mouth hung open shooting ZZZs up at the water-stained ceiling. Our eyes probed the shadows for more shotguns, knives, or anything else he might use as a weapon. A length of rope, a greasy old monkey wrench, and a honking big pair of tree loppers, all sat within his easy reach. The room's lone window, through which filtered ghostly yard light, was just a couple feet to the left of Goodman's head. In front of the window was a nightstand with an alarm clock on it, its dial glaring 5:19. Mom would start making breakfast at 6:00. Still lots of time to get back without her or dad knowing anything. Luckily, the window was open, held up by an old board. Just the outer screen stood in our way. Beyond that, I could see the *Intrepid* lying on the weathered shingles. One or both of us would have to crawl out onto the roof and get it. Miracle old man Goodman didn't wake when it crashed. Must have been a soft landing.

"I got a plan," Doreen whispered, her lips grazing my ear. "One of us climbs out onto the roof and rescues Hoppy. The other stays back to run interference on Goodman if he wakes up."

"Brilliant," whispering in her ear, the fragrance of her sweaty hair like heaven. "How do we decide who does what?"

"Rock, paper, scissors."

"Okay."

"One, two, three!"

-Scissors.

-Scissors.

"One, two, three."

-Rock.

-Paper.

"You go, dude," she whispered and then impulsively grabbed the neckline of my T-shirt, pulled me to her, and planted a big soft kiss right on my lips and then released me, smiling like I'm her hero. It was brief but long enough for her to feel my pleasurable response. "You devil... now go. I got your back. Be quick and be smart," gently shoving me into the room.

I crept in, greeted by the sound of scratching and scurrying behind the plaster walls. Doreen stayed back in the doorway. That sickly feeling of old age permeated the air and seeped into my every pore, pricking my nerves and making me weak-kneed and queasy. It put a gross taste in my mouth. Sticky. Stale. Coppery. Like an old penny that'd been sitting in the bottom of some old bag's purse since Nine-Eleven. I wanted to spit, but covered my mouth, and fought back the urge to puke. When I reached the nightstand, Goodman's head shifted so that he was looking straight up at me with his closed wrinkled eyelids and bushy white eyebrows.

He must have sensed my presence.

His gappy teeth were little more than brown stumps and his breath stunk like the dead hog pit out behind Eden Acres Hog Farm. For a minute I got the gut wrenching feeling that he was faking it. That he was really awake. Those wrinkled eyelids were open just a crack. He was watching my every move. Waiting till there was no escape. Then he'd reach up with his skeleton arms and grab me. He'd drag me out back and shoot me with that awful shotgun... .

Stop it.

The snoring stopped.

I froze. Looked back at Doreen. She was crouched down and motioned for me to do the same.

I lowered myself down until my eyes were at bed level with him.

Goodman coughed up a ball of phlegm and swallowed it back down. He reached up with his bony hand and rubbed his stubbly turkey neck, sounding like sandpaper on leather. He dropped his hand back down, flopping over the side of the cot, its long yellow nails barely missing my face.

All was still.

A minute passed.

The snoring started back up again, in spurts, like an engine having trouble getting going after sitting idle for a long time.

I cautiously stood back up, slowly reached over the nightstand, stretching my fingers out into the window, unlatched the catches on the screen, and slowly lifted it. Just a few feet away waited the *Intrepid*. I was actually going to make it. I quietly slid the alarm clock out of my way.

It read 5:30.

How did so much time go by so quickly?

Suddenly, the clock started vibrating in my hand. It started buzzing like an angry hornet in a tin can.

"What... who's that?" Goodman popped up, fumbling for his glasses on the nightstand.

I beat him to them, flinging them on the floor, buying time.

"Hurry," Doreen yelled. "Open the window. Get out."

"I can't. He'll grab me," throwing the buzzing alarm clock

at his chest. He fell back on the cot with an, "ooof," as I retreated back into the room, trapped, wanting to run.

"We can't leave Hoppy," Doreen shouted, pushing me back into the room.

My brain worked seven-miles-per-second, frantically searching for escape ideas. Then, in a McGuyver moment, I grabbed the tree loppers and the rope, wrapping one end around its long wooden handles, tying it as tight as I could.

"Who are you?" Goodman sputtered, swinging his feet around to the floor. "Pain in the ass kids. What are you doing in here? I told you kids to stay off my property."

In a suicide dash, I brushed past his grasping hands and dove through the open window, rolling onto the roof. I got up and wedged the loppers inside the window frame and repelled down the roof slope to the *Intrepid*. Grabbing my pocket knife, I pried open the rocket's nosecone.

"Hoppy," his little throat pulsating with joy. "You made it. You're alive," kissing him. He croaked back with glee. I gently put him in my T-shirt pocket. Now what? I couldn't both carry the rocket and lower myself off the roof. Tossing it to the ground would surely wake Jaws. While trying to make up my mind, Goodman's ugly face, glasses and all, popped out of the open window.

"You're that smart ass Rabnow kid aintcha?"

"Run, Doreen," I yelled, tossing the end of the rope over the edge of the roof and starting to lower myself down.

"Come back here ya little shit," tugging on the rope.

Jaws, hearing his master's voice, came running around back of the house barking up a storm, snapping at the dangling rope.

"Shep! Help!" I shouted over my shoulder toward the rock pile. "Doreen, watch out for Jaws," no idea where she'd gone.

Shep came running, met Jaws head on, engaging him in a full blown snarl and bite fest. I slid down the rope, dropping the last several feet, falling to the ground and rolling to my feet. "Doreen," I shouted, sprinting toward the river. "Let's get outta here, Shep."

A shotgun blast exploded inside the house.

"DOREEN!"

APPLY SOME PRESURE

17

Snakes tells the others he has to go use the shitter. Mongo gives him directions as to where to find the bathroom inside the house.

While sitting on the toilet he pulls out his phone, takes a selfie of his engorged member and sends it to Sage accompanied by the text, "Package received. Got this for you upon delivery. R U ready?"

A few seconds pass.

Snakes' phone dings.

"Not until you get the money," she texts back. "Had the bad luck of running into a deputy. Got served. Can you get it?"

"Fuck!," he curses to himself and sends a reply text, "Sidetracked for now. He's hooked on digging up Doreen's ghost."

"God, how long's that going to take? Sooner the banker is off my back the better."

"I'll apply some pressure… light a fire under his ass."

"Don't hurt him, for god's sake."

"C'mon, babe. I'm a brother in Christ."

"Just get the money. In the mean time I'll be warming this up for you," sending along a selfie of her pussy.

"Work it, baby. Keep it ready. The money's as good as in the bank."

On his way back out, Snakes sees Mongo's double barrel shotgun leaning in a corner by the back door. He picks it up, opens the barrels, pulls out the two shells sitting inside, inspects them, smiles maliciously, puts them back inside their chambers, and flips the barrels back in place. He searches around the kitchen and finds a roll of duct tape in a drawer, stuffs it into his jacket pocket. He picks up the gun, leans it up over his right shoulder, and struts out to rejoin to others who are still waiting out on the dock.

In the BOAT or GET WASTED

18

Snakes walks out onto the dock and levels the shotgun at both Johnny and Ariadne. Jaws drop. Richie has the Zapruder rolling, catching the action from off to the side at the far end of the T-shaped dock. Armada is standing beside him. Mongo is on the bank near the foot of the dock.

"Okay, you two," Snakes says to Johnny and Ariadne. "In the boat or get wasted."

"Snakes," Johnny says, arms outspread, taking a step toward him. "What the fuck? We got a tight shooting window. We ain't got time for this."

"Oh, this'll fit right into your script, believe me. We need to take a little visit to the real scene of the crime. Find out what really happened." Keeping the gun pointed at Johnny and Ariadne, he shouts over his shoulder, "Mongo, you still teaching back then? Media Studies? Remember what *The High Plains Dealer* had to say about old man Goodman?"

"Oh God yes. Remember it like it was yesterday. Mr. Goodman was found dead, after several days - my nephew Chris at the funeral home said his body was mush when they brought it in. But the paper was still devoting a lot of space to the search for Doreen."

"They ever determine Goodman's cause of death?" Shaking the shotgun in his hands, "Was it by one of these?"

In a flash, Snakes turns and fires at Armada's brawny breasts. The blast knocks her off the dock, splashing into the waist-deep muddy water. Everyone freaks. Screaming. Dazed and in pain, Armada threshes about but manages to get her feet planted in the soft slough bed. Her strong thick thighs lift her up out of the water, gasping for air.

"What a rush," she groans.

Richie sets the Zapruder on the dock and jumps into the water. "Armada! You're, you're not dead," feeling and examining her chest where her shirt has been shredded, the flesh of her chest and breasts pock-marked with tiny welts oozing blood.

"No, of course it wasn't by shotgun because, like Mongo's gun here, old man Goodman's was loaded with rock salt. Right, Mongo?"

Richie helps Armada wade back to the bank where Mongo helps them out of the water. Snakes picks up the Zapruder, grabs the roll of duct tape from his jacket pocket and tapes the camera to the top of the shotgun barrels. He presses the START button on the camera, points it at Johnny. He pulls the .45 out of his pants and points it, too, at Johnny.

"Okay, movie star," Snakes says. "What'd you do that night - after hearing Goodman's gun go off?"

Ariadne moves closer to Johnny, wraps her arms around his waist, whispers to him, "do what he says and we'll get through this."

Johnny, his hands up, "I, I was so shook up I blacked out. Honest, I don't recall anything but waking up in bed when I was called down for breakfast. Got a hell of a whipping from dad for being out late, for shooting off another rocket."

"Well, I'm gonna jog your memory," Snakes says, stepping closer and jabbing the .45 in Johnny's ribs. "This piece's got real bullets. In the boat. You, too, Ariadne. This second load of rock salt's got your name on it. But not yet. Not here."

"Don't do this," Ariadne says. "I have a fear of water. It doesn't have to be this way."

"Shut yer suck, cunt. Now's a good time to get over it. Move," shoving them both over to where the boat is tied.

Hiding her head in Johnny's chest, he helps her step down into the wobbly boat. He follows in after her. They sit on the middle seat, facing towards the boat's motor. Snakes stuffs the .45 back into his pants, unties the boat and gets in, setting the shotgun/camera down in the boat's belly for the moment. He uses an oar to push off from the dock, pull-starts the little old motor, and they putter off upstream toward the Goodman place.

NEAR DEATH EXPERIENCE

19

They pass under the Wilkin Avenue bridge and go another quarter mile up to a bend in the slough, just before the Goodman place.

"This is about where it happened," Snakes says. "Ain't it, Ariadne?"

She's too traumatized to answer. She flashes back thirteen years to when she was on the high school cross country ski team. They were out practicing on the frozen slough. When they came upon the bend, she unexpectedly hit a patch of thin ice (due to the strong under current). She broke through - completely submerged. The end of one of her ski poles hooked a crook in the broken ice, preventing the strong current from carrying her away. The ski pole's leather thong, looped around her wrist, allowed her to hang on. She was only under a matter of seconds, but time seemed to stop. She opened her eyes, gazing deep into the dark swirling depths. Into oblivion. She panicked with the fear of being pulled in. But something inside her, a voice, told her to relax and let go - it would be better down there. She actually did loosen her grip and let go of the ski pole. But the thong held onto her. The voice - more felt than heard - more irresistible, told her to relax and she could be free. She began to feel her hand slip through the thong. But then, her wrist felt squeezed as if in a vice. A jolt ran up her arm as she was pulled up out of the water. A teammate, Amanda Miller, was saving her. Other team members, all blurs in the white frosty air, rushed from the sides to help - grasping her hands, helping pull. Amanda, her best friend, *cannot live without her*, reached into the water, grabbed for a knee to pull it out. Amanda slipped and fell in. The current took her. She was never found.

"A couple of years before Hollywood's rocket incident," Snakes continues. "Wasn't it? While your team members searched for poor Amanda, you went to the nearest house to dry off and warm up. It was Goodman's house. What did you see there? What did you two do?"

The GOODMAN HOUSE

20

Snakes kills the boat motor and coasts up onto the muddy bank along Goodman's land. He picks up the shotgun-mounted camera, gets it rolling and prods Johnny and Ariadne to get out and trod through the weedy yard up to the abandoned house. It's sat vacant ever since the old man died ten years back, a ghost of itself: weathered grey wood siding completely stripped of paint, one corner of the roof caved in from heavy snow, windows broken out, porch over-grown with vines and tree branches, front door hanging by one hinge.

Johnny manhandles the door, lifting it off the floorboards, pushing it screeching into the kitchen. Looking around, cautiously, he leads the way inside. Rubble strewn everywhere. Filthy table and ratty vinyl kitchen chairs.

"Someone's been here," Johnny says, pointing to footprints on the dusty linoleum-covered floor.

"Not surprised," Snakes says. "Place is a hangout for juvies and junkies.

"You would know," Ariadne says.

"Shut the fuck up and walk," jabbing the shotgun into her back.

They side-step their way through the debris and pass through a doorway into what looks to have been a living room: sunk-in couch discolored by dirt and stains, antique wooden rocker with a busted armrest, cast iron potbelly stove, trash everywhere, mildew crawling up the tattered green floral wallpaper (plaster and lathes showing through in places), slight undertone smell of shit and decay.

"Bring back memories?" Snakes smiles sarcastically.

"Wasn't in much better shapes that night," Johnny says.

"Not as good as I remember it," Ariadne says.

"So I've been told, the old man's remains were discovered in that room over there," Snakes points to a partially opened door at the far end of the living room.

Johnny opens the door and leads them into a bedroom: antique dresser with a huge broken mirror perched above it, four poster bed with a nauseating stain on its mattress. The closet's sliding doors sit open. Its empty except for the feotul-shaped carcass lying on the floor - white bones and patches of parchment skin and fur. Probably a deer, died seeking shelter from the cold many winters back.

"My guess," Johnny says. "He bought the farm in here. On that bed. That's his stain."

"I knew him," Ariadne says, her voice hitching. She covers her face with her hand. Takes a moment to compose herself. Then continues. "Contrary to his reputation, he was a kind man. When I fell through the slough he was out feeding the chickens he kept in his back yard. He saw the whole thing and rushed down with a heavy wool army blanket. I was shivering so bad. He wrapped it around me and guided me up to his house. Got me undressed - I let him do it, imagining myself in the scene in the movie *Vertigo* where Scotty pulls Madeline out of San Fransisco Bay, takes her home, undresses her, and puts her to bed. Like Scotty, Goodman was my savior. He gave me a robe to wear and hung my wet clothes to dry by the wood burning stove out there in the kitchen. This bedroom was a lot nicer back then. Had an old world Victorian charm. He tucked me into this very same bed," sitting down on an unstained edge and running her hand along the mattress. I was still shaking. In shock. He was sensitive to that fact," she pauses again, her shoulders convulsing. A tear runs down her cheek. "He got undressed and crawled in bed with me, warming me with his body. My shivers subsided and I fell asleep. When I awoke in the morning he was still with me, his arms wrapped around me. It was the most secure feeling I had ever had. I let him make love to me - sodomize me. It's not what you think. That image of oblivion from under the slough was still swirling through the back of my head. Even though you may view what he did as perverted and sick, he was a human being touching me. I let him have me. Feeling him inside me chased the oblivion away. Afterwards, he gave me hot chocolate and made me breakfast. We became friends. I'd come over at least once a week, every week, for a year after that, until I graduated and moved to Minneapolis for college. He showed me things no one else knew about him. He was a Thelemite - a disciple of Aleister Crowley. He taught me the secret rituals of sexual Magick.

"He was a beast," Snakes says, leaning against a decrepit dresser, eyeing her with loathing. "He used you."

"He wasn't the first," shooting daggers back at him.

"Let's not get personal here," Johnny says, pacing the small bedroom, his eyes searching the scattered debris. "We need to look for clues."

"As his disciple," Snakes says, breaking his stare-down with Ariadne and walking around tapping the wood-paneled walls with his knuckles. "You should know if he had a lair.

Some secret chamber with pentagrams and shit, an altar to fuck you on and all."

"You've seen too many B movies," Ariadne says, rising up off the mattress. "But he did have a secret room," walking toward the large double closet. "It's in here."

The closet space is completely bare except for the deer carcass and some trash lying on the floor. Ariadne steps inside and feels around along one side of its back wall. She digs a fingernail into a crevice in the paneling and pries back a section. Pulls it from the wall and sets it aside, revealing a small hidden door made of rough-cut barn wood. She crouches down and pushes on the door. It's hinges creek and reluctantly gives inward, leaving in its place a gaping black rectangular hole four feet high and three wide.

BLONDE BUDDHA

21

By memory, Ariadne crouches down and feels her way into the dark portal. But it's been twelve years. She senses things inside the room have changed. Johnny is crunched behind her. She twists her head back and holds out her palm to him, "No lights in there. May I have your Zippo?"

He digs it out of his pocket, flips it open, lights it and carefully hands it forward. The lighter casts an eerie flickering dirty glow to the small chamber. Ariadne crawls through the doorway and then is able to stand fully erect.

Before Johnny enters, he turns back to Snakes who has the shotgun camera rolling, "Don't even think of bringing that thing in. It won't pick up anything in this dim light."

"Obviously," leaning it against a closet corner. "But I still got the .45 so don't try anything fancy."

Johnny crawls into the chamber behind Ariadne and Snakes follows him.

The room is very much like Ariadne remembers. She slowly walks to where she remembers two large candles sat on an altar. Their forms materialize out of the darkness as she draws near them. She lights each and more of the twelve foot-square windowless room becomes visible. The walls are covered in blood-red stucco. A pentagram has been painted on the hardwood floor. All eyes are drawn to a small platform by the far wall. Sitting on it, in the lotus position, there appears to be an almost life-size statue of a buddha.

Looking at it, Johnny appears to be frozen in some kind of trance.

It was not in the room when Ariadne was last there. She flips the cover closed on the Zippo, stuffs it back into Johnny's pocket, and picks up one of the candles from the altar, takes Johnny's hand and slowly leads him to the buddha. Snakes grabs the other candle and follows along, interested in checking out this pagan idolatry shit so he can refute it. The statue takes on a golden glow as they draw near, its features growing more distinct, more life-like than the world's greatest artist could render. It's not a statue at all, but a young blonde girl.

Johnny falls to his knees and kisses the bare foot of the girl. "Doreen. At last. Oh, poor, poor, girl." His tears fall and glisten on the shellacked surface of the small foot.

Ariadne and Snakes look on, both speechless at the horrible sight of this thin little girl's mummified corpse. Her shiny mottled flesh having been preserved by several coats of wood varnish.

Ariadne kneels beside Johnny, placing a tender hand on his shoulder. "Oh, Johnny, I'm so sorry."

He flinches, startled out of his trance, lifts his head and lets Ariadne pull it into her embrace, resting it on her breasts, absorbing his convulsive sobs.

Snakes walks around the room, studying it. Hanging on one wall is an Egyptian stele - a 12"x24" board covered with gesso showing the pantheon of ancient Egyptian gods, their story told in hieroglyphs. On a table he finds something puzzling. A model rocket. He picks it up. Looks it over.

"What the fuck is this doing in here?" Walking it over to Johnny. "Yours, ain't it? The one you shot off over Goodman's house."

Johnny lifts his head and stands, takes the rocket, turns it in his hands... contemplates. "Fuckin right it is. Rabnow must have found it. He did all this. I'm gonna kill that fucker."

"This is a major break," Ariadne says. "But how would he have known about the room? And how would it explain him preserving Doreen seated like a Buddha? Rabnow doesn't seem the Buddhist type."

"Maybe a Chinese invader did it," Snakes says.

"Doreen died long before they came along. Had to be someone who worshipped her. Someone who, it appears, was damn good with wood... ."

Ariadne and Snakes both glare at Johnny.

"What? Don't give me that look. I'm just a hack compared to Rabnow."

"Take it easy. We know that's impossible," Ariadne says, leaning down to examine some flowers sitting in a vase beside Doreen. "Are these real? They are. They're in water. Wilted but the petals are still soft. Someone's been here... just a day or two ago."

"The killer. Our psycho. We need to come back with lights and film this."

"And dust for prints," Ariadne says.

"Won't need em," Snakes says, bringing over a small leather bound book he found on the same table the rocket had been on. "Check this out," opening the book and reading its title page. *"The DEVOTIONAL JOURNAL of JORDY RABNOW."*

"Knew it had to be that pervert," Johnny says. "He was always hitting on Doreen back in school. They were cousins for fuck sake."

"Fucking incestuous perv. Get this, from what I remember hearing, crazy fucker deflowered her on a combine - *while combining*."

Johnny's face turns beet-red, "That's fucking bullshit!"

"Well, let's see if Jordy himself has anything to say about it," taking the journal from Snakes. She flips through it, finds an entry and reads.

JORDY'S JOURNAL

22

Dad taught me how to drive the Super 92 today.

The Massey Ferguson Super 92 combine is a huge mechanical monster; 11 feet wide, 25 feet long, and 12 feet tall. It is an antique piece of Americana from the glory days of family farming in the 1950s. My dad's is faded red with speckles of rust. When it's in the heat of operation, it growls and gnashes its teeth like an angry beast and often, like an obstinate mule, it breaks down, refusing to do your bidding. Dad only uses it because he can't afford anything more modern. And, he's obsessed with Masseys.

The ripe wheat has been cut and swathed into rows ready for combining (dad did it a couple days ago).

So I'm sitting high up on the operator's platform, overlooking the rows as the combine slowly gobbles them up. Dad clings to the small platform's ladder with one powerful fist clenching its inch-thick iron tube railing. He gives me a quick tutorial of all the Super 92's controls; an array of medieval-looking iron levers sticking out at odd angles from a panel on the other side of my seat.

He has me make one round - combining a row of wheat all the way down the quarter-mile-length field. At the end, I make a u-turn and come back, combining the next row, all at a snail's pace.

Just as we finished the round and turned to make another, we see the Norde's car kicking up dust coming up our long gravel driveway. It pulls off into the grassy yard headed toward the nearby garden.

It's my uncle and aunt and cousin Doreen, who's my same age. I'm bummed that I'm stuck in the combine because Doreen and I like to hangout together.

"Looks like you got the hang of it," dad says. "Make another round on your own."

Dad hops off the ladder and walks across the wheat stubble to go chat with the Nordes who are piling out of their car, getting ready to tend their tomatoes, peas, carrots and corn.

I see Doreen see me and get excited to see her come running over. She reaches the combine in no time, grabs the platform ladder and climbs aboard.

"Got room for a stowaway, captain?" she says, panting, smiling like sunshine. She squeezes onto the tiny platform and leans against the guard rail beside me.

"Yup. But it'll cost ya."

She's changed since I last saw her two months ago, on the last day of school. She's wearing tight cutoff jeans and a soiled pink halter top which is tight enough that I get a good eyeful of her budding womanhood. It's hard for me to keep my eyes on my driving. I'm afraid she might notice the attention I'm giving them. But, what if she does, and she likes it? I feel excited in a new but weird way.

We combine along in silence for a few minutes.

"Jeez," Doreen says, getting tired of watching. "Don't hog all the fun." She twists her slender body and slides in between me and the combine's iron steering wheel. "Scootch your butt back and show me how you work this thing."

She plops her tiny hiny down on my lap. I slide back tight up against the seat's backrest, spreading my legs wide to give her a bit *of the vinyl padded seat. My heart's pounding like a jackhammer. I'm wearing cargo shorts, so my bare legs are pressed against her soft bare legs. I've never felt anything so heavenly.*

To avoid running off a wheat row, I depress the clutch pedal with my left foot, stopping the Super 92 dead in its tracks.

"Okay," I tell her. "Now put your foot on top of mine."

She does so, giggling. "Hey, are you trying to play footsie with me?"

"Not quite. Now I'm going to slide my foot away. When I do, you slowly lift yours to get the combine moving again."

Doreen lets out the clutch so fast that the machine lurches forward, thrusting my body forward against hers. My face plunges into her fresh strawberry scented hair. I'm shocked to find I've got an erection. I try to will it to go down but can't. In fact, just thinking about how wrong this all is makes it even harder.

"This thing ain't got power steering. I'd better help you steer," placing my hands on top of hers on the steering wheel.

The powerful threshing motion of the combine causes everything to vibrate, including my sensitive inexperienced organ, making it jiggle against Doreen's backside. Makes me spasm like jello. I can't believe I'm in love with my cousin. But I can't help it and I've never felt better in my life. I can't resist kissing her neck.

"What are you doing?" turning her head and giving me a surprised look. She feels the wetness and looks down to see the stain in my shorts and her look turns to disgust. "Ew, Jordy, you're gross."

The combine veers off course, angling across several wheat rows. Dad sees it and comes running after us, shouting for me to stop.

"Enough," Johnny says, grabbing the journal from Ariadne and closing it. "We get the picture."

"What now, boss?" she says.

"No brainer," Snakes says. "Rabnow has gotta be hiding out at his farm. I say we go out and cap his ass," fingering his .45.

"My sentiments exactly," Johnny says.

"Let's not get ahead of ourselves," Ariadne says. "America's Next Great Psycho is an hour-long show. With barely fifteen minutes worth of film shot, we need another couple scenes to draw out the suspense and build tension."

Johnny turns and gazes sadly down at Doreen. "Let's seal this room back up," letting out a heavy sigh and laying Jordy's journal at her feet. "We'll come back later with lights. Catch it on film. But, right now, I could go for a good stiff drink. Who's for hitting *The Old Mill*?"

YOU GIVE ME JORDY and I'LL GIVE YOU TARA

23

Johnny, Ariadne (blindfolded to cope with her fear of water), and snakes motorboat half a mile up stream to *The Old Mill*.

The three-story structure, built in 1888, was originally a flour mill that ground wheat for the area farmers. The BROFO Motorcycle Club purchased the dilapidated property in 2005 to use as a clubhouse. Bit by bit, over the years, they restored it and, in 2015, the bar and restaurant opened for business. In 2020 they got the giant water wheels spinning again, using them to power the club's Bible printing and binding operation in the building's upper floors.

Snakes ties-up their boat at the mill-side dock and climbs out. Johnny helps Ariadne out and unties her blindfold. They weave their way through the tables of outside diners, making their way to the restaurant's side door. Inside, a flour mill theme dominates the decor: huge white grindstones serve as tables and antique farm tools adorn the barn wood-covered walls.

It's busy, but Snakes uses his pull to score them a corner

table overlooking the churning waters. Johnny orders a Hamms on tap, Ariadne a daiquiri, and Snakes Jack and coke. He also orders an appetizer platter of beer batter breaded catfish nuggets (caught fresh off the dock) for everyone.

They relax with a little small talk about what a great place it is and then Snakes gets down to business.

"Before you *off* Jordy, I need something from him."

"Like what," Johnny says, chain-popping catfish nuggets into his mouth. "Is it something we should include in the show?"

"It's a little matter of one hundred thousand dollars," throwing back his Jack.

"What?" washing down his nuggets with a gulp of Hamms. "That perv is just poor white trash. He aim't got that kind of dough."

"Keep your voice down," looking over at the two BROFOs tending bar. "My biker brothers don't know about this and, trust me, you don't want them to."

"Snakes?" Ariadne says, wondering what's up.

"Grab your drinks and follow me," he says, sliding his chair back. "Want to show you something."

He leads them through a door at the end of the bar and up a narrow flight of creaky time-worn wooden steps emerging on the second floor where the BROFOS print and bind their special blue-letter Bibles. The large open rafter-girded room has retained its rustic pioneer feel exuding an effluvium of dry grain and airplane glue.

Snakes flips a switch and hanging bare bulbs glow orange. Bulky medieval-grade machines sit greased and waiting: a torturous-looking book press, linotype machine with congealed molten lead splattered on the plank-wood floor around it, a grease and ink-stained California job case, ink press, and workbenches.

"A lot of this stuff we got from *The High Plains Dealer*," Snakes explains. "After they modernized their print room."

"How does all this involve Jordy?" Ariadne asks.

"His old man was a scientific genius. We hired him to invent the special blue ink for our Bibles. We call it Crystal Blue Redemption because it's 94.2 percent pure crystal meth. Back in April gave him a hundred grand worth of meth to make a new batch of ink. The old man suddenly gets the virus. Couple weeks later he kicks the bucket. Month later Jordy disappears. Probably fenced the meth in Minneapolis. Searched his farm high and low. No sign of the money, or anything fancy that he might of spent it on. When I get my hands on him I'm gonna wring the truth out of him."

"I heard that his mom was concerned that Jordy was dead, not having heard from him since he left."

"Where'd you hear that, Ariadne," Johnny says.

"Never mind," shaking her head. "Just speculating."

"The money's not for me," Snakes says. "It's for his mom. Bank is fixing to foreclose on her house. She's a good woman and I'd do anything for her."

Johnny gulps the rest of his beer and throws the empty glass at a printing press spraying glass across the wood plank floor.

"You son-of-a-bitch," he shouts, grabbing Snakes' t-shirt. "You've been playing me all along."

"That's right," shoving him away. "I know where Tara is, *Johnny*. You give me Jordy so I can get the money, and I'll give you Tara."

Johnny, fuming, rushes Snakes, hits him in the jaw and knocks him to the floor.

On his back, Snakes pulls the .45 on him, keeping him at bay. Ariadne rushes to shield Johnny.

Snakes' phone comes alive with its *Amazing Grace* ring tone. Keeping the pistol pointed at Ariadne and Johnny, he pulls it out of his jacket pocket and checks it.

"Excuse me, gotta take this," lodging the phone between his shoulder and cheek. He answers the call, "Yeah, ma... . Not yet but getting there... uhuh... sounds good... . I'm fucking starving. We all are... . You bet. See ya soon, love," putting the phone away. He announces, "We're all invited over to Jordy's mom's for supper."

DINER WITH SAGE

24

A dirty white Ford Winstar minivan with rusty wheel wells and *Old Mill Catering* on its doors lumbers down dusty Main Street. Old Bill (delivering an order of beer and pizza) is driving. Snakes rides shotgun. Scrunched in beside the *goods* on the back seat are Johnny and Ariadne.

Dusk is descending. Neon signs for the bowling alley and Earl's Corner Bar blink to life. A few cars and pickups are parked out front of each. Otherwise, the town looks deserted. Passing by Earl's, its front door being propped open, they get a blast of loud redneck music punctuated with gunshots.

"Sounds like a good ole ass whooping," Johnny says.

"Forgot to tell you about the *killing bars*," Snakes says.

"Please, enlighten us," Ariadne says. "What are the *killing bars*?"

"Bars officially recognized by the Chinese - one in each town - where killing is legal. No questions asked. Places where the locals can vent. Convenient way for the Chinese occupation government to weed out troublemakers."

"Seems like their intel," Johnny says. "Comes from

watching old westerns."

"These bars sound like an enter-at-your-own-risk type deal," Ariadne says.

"You got it," Snakes says. "The cops got no jurisdiction inside a killing bar. Long as what goes on is within a fifty foot radius of the building, or inside the bar itself - they can't touch you."

"That settles it," Johnny says. "We're fucking going."

"Yeah," Snakes says. "Right up your alley, after we drop in on Mrs. Rabnow. She's gonna kill us all if we're not knocking on her back door like, right now."

The driver takes a right on Wilkin Avenue, crosses over the bridge and then hangs another right on the first street after the slough.

"What else is new," Johnny says,

"I shit you not," Snakes says. "They've banned cheese of all odors and varieties."

"They got something against cheese?"

"Swear to God, gotta go up to Canada to get a cheeseburger. The cheese on that pizza back there is contraband. That's a highly illegal pizza we're delivering." Snakes motions to the driver, "That's it up on the right, the one with the white columns."

Ariadne whispers to Johnny, "Don't forget, you're Johnny fucking Wonder."

"I'm trying," Johnny says softly back to her. "Really hard to keep that in mind, Ariadne."

The delivery van pulls into a long shady driveway that curves around to a side door near the back, slough side, of the house. The driver pulls to a stop behind Sage's Jeep SUV parked right up to the door. Snakes grabs the shotgun. Johnny grabs the pizza. All three pile out and the driver backs the van out, returning to the *Old Mill*.

"If Jordy's inside," Snakes says. "Distract him with the pizza and I'll butt-slap his puss," making a swift uppercut with the butt of the shotgun. He digs in his pocket for a key and unlocks the back door. "After you," holding the door open for Johnny and Ariadne.

They step into a narrow dark, precariously-stacked boxes-of-junk-lined entrance way leading into the kitchen. Snakes closes and locks the door behind him and follows them in, flipping on the kitchen light. More clutter: kitchen gadgets, utensils, shopping bags full of dry goods, already-read newspapers spilling off the table onto the litter-carpeted floor. They have to shuffle sideways, like crabs, to get through.

"Sage's rule of the house," Snakes announces. "Everyone washes their hands before they do anything else."

Johnny drops the pizza box on top of the mound of newspapers, magazines and mail covering the round oak dining table. Snakes sets the shotgun down behind the door and steps over to the sink (barely visible under stacks of dirty dishes), shoos away the hovering fruit flies, washes his hands with a squirt of antibacterial hand soap, dries them with a dish towel grabbed from the oven door handle, rubs them with a shot of hand sanitizer, and steps aside for Ariadne to repeat the routine.

"So," Johnny says. "What kind of dame is this Mrs. Rabnow?"

"She ain't no *dame*," Snakes retorts. "She's a saint. A woman of high moral fiber. The kind that are so rare these days. And don't you go stealing her away," shaking a fist in his face.

"Don't worry," Ariadne says. "I have Johnny boy on a very tight leash," turning away from the sink. She smirks and winks at Johnny and flicks her wet fingers at his face. He sticks out his tongue at her and flips her the bird.

"That fits right in with Jordy's psycho profile," Johnny

says. "Most serial killers come from strict moral upbringings," stepping over to the sink and washing his hands.

"The hell ya say," Snakes says.

"He's right," Ariadne says. "Parental forced moral rectitude acts like a compression chamber for the young psycho's developing libido. His desire is like a ticking bomb. Then, when the right stimulus hits him, WAMMO! The result is devastating."

"Well, let's go see if the psycho is home," Snakes says, grabbing a stack of five plates from the cupboard. "Grab that pizza and follow me."

He heads for a dark doorway in the kitchen's far wall. Johnny wipes his hands, picks up the pizza, and he and Ariadne follow him into the living room. Some ten feet in, beyond shadowy mounds of waist-high clutter, the cackle of a TV game show and a crack of flickering blue light emanates from a half-open door.

They crab-walk single file navigating a treacherous path through the thrift store junk. Johnny throws an ominous glance up a dark set of stairs they pass along the way. Snakes stops at the bedroom door and gives it a *Beethoven's Fifth* series of taps.

The TV is suddenly muted and they hear a barely audible, brink-of-death reply, "Ye-e-es?"

Snakes nudges the door open. It'll only go halfway because of the boxes of shit piled behind it.

"Hey ma, you got visitors."

Ariadne, leans around from behind Johnny and Snakes, "Mrs. Rabnow, I'm Ariadne, agent of TV star Johnny Wonder," grabbing Johnny and pulling his head into view beside hers. "Thank you for inviting us into your lovely home."

Sage is painted a flickering pale neon blue by the big flat

screen TV (the room's only light source) mounted on the wall beyond the foot of her bed, the wall through which her visitors are looking. She is lying on her bed in a red velvet bathrobe, halfway open, barely covering her large breasts. Her long iron-grey hair is a rat's nest halo around her pillowed head. A bedding of thoroughly studied newspapers surrounds her short fit figure. A bed-side nightstand is over-burdened with all the necessities: full ashtray, highball glass of vodka Fresca on ice, heavily notated legal pad, pens, cellphone, TV remote, and a well-thumbed black leather Bible. The air is warm and stuffy; reeking of cigarettes, booze, and sweat.

Sage props herself up on one elbow, reaches over for the highball, takes a long drink, and replaces the glass. She glares at them, "Have you thoroughly washed and sanitized your hands?" her voice stronger, raspy. "I won't have that virus in my house."

"Yes, ma-am," Johnny says. "Both Ariadne and I are uncontaminated."

"What are you doing out galavanting around during a travel ban?"

"They're making a TV show, ma."

"Lord Almighty. Had I known I'd be entertaining celebrities I'd have gotten all dolled-up," fishing for a hairbrush in the nightstand drawer. She finds it and brushes her long kinky tresses. "What kind of show?"

"I'm sure you've heard of it," Ariadne says. "America's Next Great Psycho. We track down fugitive serial killers and bring them to justice."

"That's right, ma-am," Johnny says. "And I hate to bring this to you, but we've found solid evidence that your son, Jordy, was responsible...," his voice hitches as his eyes lower to the filthy carpet. He pauses, regains his composure and locks onto her blood-shot eyes. "Responsible for the death of

Doreen Norde. And that's why we're here, ma-am, hoping you can lead us to his where-a-bouts."

Sage slaps the hairbrush down hard on the matted newspapers, "You have the nerve to come into my house with the intent to kill my darling boy!?"

"I am truly sorry, ma-am, but th, that does seem to be the truth of the matter."

Sage pushes her blanket away and pulls herself up into a sitting position, crossing her legs underneath her, her robe parting into the territory of the dangerously obscene. She takes a cigarette from the pack on the nightstand, lights it, takes a drag, and blows out a long plume of blue smoke at the ceiling.

"Well, come in. Find a place to sit. Let's talk this thing over."

One-by-one they crowd into the electric blue twilight, right up alongside Sage's bed, setting the plates, pizza, and beer down on the mattress at her feet like an offering. Johnny glances over at the overly stuffed closet: lingerie, leather biker gear bearing the BROFO emblem, slinky dresses, rumpled jeans, bras, panties laying in a heap.

"You ride with the BROFOs, ma-am?"

"I'm the club's Mother Superior," flashing a lurid smile. "Queen bitch of the Burning Heart and Cross," winking at him. "Wanna join our gang? I haven't bathed in days. Just for you, honey," spreading her knees even wider, the part in her robe climbing dangerously up the muscled contours of her strong naked thighs. She smiles lewdly into his eyes. "Smell my cunt?"

Underneath the cigarette and booze stench, Johnny gets a whiff of something sweet and sickly - like wilting honeysuckle. Looking around the room, he sees no flowers. The corner of his mouth twitches, his nose involuntarily scrunches up. He feels slimed.

Snakes whacks him up back the head, causing him to fall forward. He braces himself with a hand on the bed to prevent himself from falling into her lap and the prospect of involuntary cunnilingus.

"Be polite. Answer ma's question."

Ariadne kicks the back of Snakes' knee, causing him to fall backwards against a dresser. "That's no way to treat the star of a TV show."

"Whoa. Whoa. Whoa," Sage shouts. "What the fuck? Everyone just settle the fuck down. I won't have rudeness in this house."

Johnny and Snakes each regain their balance, standing back up.

"My apologies, Mrs. Rabnow," Johnny says. " But you are very, pardon the phrase, seductive… ."

"Why, thank you, hun," granting him a patronizing smile while staring deep into his eyes. "A divorce lawyer once tried to serve me. I fucked his brains out and shoved the papers up his ass."

"That's very impressive," Ariadne says. "But, we need to ask you about Jordy, if we may."

"Certainly. My loving son is my favorite topic of conversation. Please, everyone, find a seat," patting the bed beside her. "I don't know about you, but I'm famished. It'll be more tasty to discuss him while we enjoy this nice pizza. You, my dear," reaching for Johnny's hand. "Can sit right close where I can feast my eyes upon you."

Johnny sits down on the middle of the bed.

"Oh, come on. You can do better than that."

He slides slightly closer.

"I won't cooperate if you don't," patting the bed beside her. "Come, don't be shy. You're a big boy now. I won't bite."

He exhales deeply, raises his eyes to the water-stained ceiling tiles, and slides all the way up to the head of the bed next to her.

Ariadne, observing intently, sits down on a small vanity chair at the foot of the bed.

Snakes, smirking, sits on the foot of the bed and dishes out the pizza and beer.

"Just one plate for us," Sage says. "Hollywood and I can share, hun."

Snakes loads a plate with a couple slices and hands it up to her. She takes it, picks up a slice and holds it over to Johnny's face. It's hot and smells yummy. He takes a bite. She pulls the piece away from his mouth and uses a finger to break a stringer of cheese. She twirls it around her finger and pushes it into his mouth. He sucks her finger clean. She uses her fingernail to scrape the tomato paste from his lips and brings the finger to her own mouth and sucks it clean with a loud smacking sound. She then takes a bite from the same slice of pizza.

Snakes and Ariadne eat and watch, amused.

Johnny scowls and washes down the nicotine taste of her finger with a swig of beer. "Tell me, Mrs. Rabnow," he says. "When you took your tit away from Jordy, with what did he replace it?"

"He never had it. I bottle fed him. You want it now?" taking his hand, she slips it into her robe and holds it over her bare left breast. It's hard but warm and full.

"That just may be what turned him into a sex psycho," tweaking her hard nipple. "His perversions compensate for the intimacy you never gave him," narrowing his eyes at her and squeezing her breast. He curls in his upper lip, baring his teeth, and makes obscene slurpy-sucking sounds at her.

Pissed, Snakes throws his half-eaten pizza slice at his face. Johnny retrieves his hand and ducks, the pizza splattering the wall behind the bed.

"Show some respect."

Sage, screaming at the top of her lungs, "Everyone calm the fuck down. Eat your pizza." She turns to Johnny, takes a deep breath, lets out a long sigh and says with restrained calm, "That was very naughty. Something you learned in Hollywood, no doubt. I'll have to give you sone obedience training," shaking her finger in his face.

"I promise to behave."

"Good," patting his thigh, then sliding it up inside and squeezing. "So tell me, psycho hunter, if I give Jordy my breast will he come home?"

"Are you saying he's not here?"

"How should I know? How can you tell a psycho?"

"We ask them four special questions," Ariadne says. "How many people have you killed? How many Chinese are after you? How many times have you seen your mother naked? And, which of these question have you lied about? We observe their physiological responses: ticks, tells, respiration, body language. True sociopaths can't hide it."

"I see," Sage says. "You bring him home to me and you won't have to kill him."

"Well," Johnny says. "Problem is, that's not the kind of climax I'm looking for… for, for the show.

Sage and Snakes exchange looks.

Johnny and Ariadne exchange looks.

"Will you please excuse me," Johnny says. "The little boys room is calling."

"Of course, my dear," removing her hand from his thigh.

Johnny, slightly flushed, stands and turns toward the door.

"Just off the kitchen on the left," Snakes says.

"I know where it is," Johnny says, stepping on his toe in passing.

"Back in five," shoving him toward the doorway. "Before the pizza gets cold."

"Shut up and eat." Johnny grabs Ariadne's arm and says to

her, "Looks like your nose needs powdering."
    She excuses herself, gets up, and follows him out.

BATHROOM STRATEGY SESSION

25

Johnny and Ariadne squeeze into the bathroom, tramping on used magazines and avoiding dirty dishes (Ariadne has to struggle to get the door closed behind them). Johnny lifts the scuzzy toilet seat up with his foot, pulls down his fly and relieves himself, loud as a race horse from the former Soviet Union.

"That scene was fucking nauseating," he says. "What a fucking whore. You know she left Jordy's dad for that low-life?"

"Where did you hear that?" gazing down, admiring Johnny's piece.

"It's obvious. *Why* is the question."

"She's an addict. You saw that Bible on the night stand."

"He said he'd give me Tara for Jordy. What the fuck was that all about?"

"He's bluffing. Just wants that money he thinks Jordy's hiding."

"Which means Jordy's not here?"

"Jordy is probably hiding on his dad's farm. We should

leave. Get away from these drug addicts while we can."

"I agree. But, since we're here, I'd like to take a look upstairs. There's a chance he may still have a room up there that could give us valuable insight on him."

"True, but... ."

"You go back in, stall them. Tell them I'm nauseous - might have the virus."

"I don't like it. We need to go while we can."

Johnny finally finishes. Shakes off, zips up, and turns to her.

"What's the matter? You jealous of that horny old slut?"

Ariadne reaches down and grabs his tight ass, pulling him close, husky whisper as she tongues his ear, "Funny guy."

Johnny smiles and pushes her back. "You're jealous. Don't worry. I'll be back to rescue you before things get hairy," opening the door for her. "Now get back in there and wow them with that high powered brain, sweet puss," slapping her tiny ass.

JORDY'S ROOM

26

After leaving the bathroom, Johnny takes a left at the stairs just inside the living room doorway. He silently climbs the carpeted steps, careful to avoid creaks that might give him away. Upon reaching the dark landing at the top, he stops, listens, and takes a quick look around. The doors of two rooms stand open, their entrances blocked by mounds of chest-high shit. Obviously no one in there. At the far end of the twenty-foot-long landing, a third door is closed. If anything, that would have to be Jordy's room.

Johnny cautiously moves toward it, carful not to knock over any junk along the way. The door is the antique kind with a time-worn brass knob and keyhole beneath. A pale light emanates from the keyhole. He kneels and peeps through it.

"Tara," his heart skipping.

He withdraws his face, rubs his eye and looks again. He sees her again. Most upsetting of all, a sees a large bullhead lurking in front of her. Fuming, Johnny twists the knob and bursts into the room.

He stops in the doorway.

He'd fallen for someone's trick, an optical illusion. What he saw of Tara was only an 8x10 glass framed photo of her. It's sitting atop a waist-high dresser canted at a 45 degree angle toward the doorway. At that angle the picture-frame-glass catches the reflection off a mirror hanging on the half-open closet door. The mirror, in turn, is reflecting an image from the half-tilted-open window glass. Which, in turn, is reflecting the image of the huge bullhead painted on the town water tower which stands just a few blocks away. The bullhead on the water tower is catching the last golden rays of the sunken sun.

The only other light in the room is the soft glow of a night light plugged into a low wall socket.

Johnny picks up the photo, his breath catching. It's not a normal photo of Tara. Her face is tear-streaked, gripped in pain. A red bandana is cinched tight across her mouth.

"Fucker really has her," he mutters, choked up. "You're fucking taunting me. Bullhead's your fucking… your fucking power animal. You lined all this shit up on purpose… perfectly… just to spite me… to leave your stain on her."

Johnny sets the photo face down on the dresser top and looks around the room. In stark contrast to the rest of the house, completely empty except for a couple things; the dresser, a beat-up kid's desk, and twin bed with a bare mattress.

To calm himself, he takes a slow deep breath. He detects the lingering odor of honeysuckle and something more acrid, like gunpowder.

"She's been in here today."

This room is where Jordy had pined-away all his adolescent troubles. He picks up on the vibes of the accumulated heartaches emanating from the yellowed wallpaper. Where was his secret hiding place? His hidden stash hole?

He turns toward the dresser, kneels and pulls its bottom drawer all of the way out from its frame and sets it aside on the carpeted floor. He reaches into the dark cavity under where the drawer had been and feels around. Bingo. He pulls out a leather bound journal. *Jordy's secret confessions!* He reaches into his pocket, pulls out his Zippo. Flips it open and flicks it to life. He pages through the journal, comes upon taped-in cut-out pics from newspapers and school yearbooks. They are all of some young brunette hottie. A post-Doreen obsession? He flips past the pages of pics and comes upon sealed Ziplock baggies taped to a page. Preserved inside one baggie is a lock of long dark hair. Inside a second baggie is a tangle of dark pubic hair. *Another victim!*

After the baggies are several pages of what look like diary entries. Johnny pages through them to the end. Strangely, the last entry looks all marked-up with annotations and editing notations. Johnny reads.

JORDY'S HIGH SCHOOL JOURNAL

27

I get home from school feeling like shit. I slam the kitchen door shut and drop my backpack on a stool by the sink. Mom is taking a tray of sizzling buffalo chicken wings out of the oven. She looks flustered.

"Sup, mom?"

"Hi, honey. We have company. Please wash-up. Supper's almost ready."

Company is the last thing I'm in the mood for. I need mom's sympathetic ear to help with my girl problems. I head straight for my room, flop down on my bed, the lovely image of the most beautiful girl in school, CODI SOUTHERN, floats through my head. But the image is stained. It's crowded out by that ugly smirking crater-faced ASSHOLE.

It's been one of the worst days of my life. THE ASSHOLE, who has no business being at the school since he's not even a student, has been showing up a lot lately - always at the end of the school day. Today was no exception. THE ASSHOLE held CODI's hand - both of them laughing - as he walked her out to his car. They walked right by me and she completely ignored me.

CODI's the first girl to capture my love since I lost DOREEN all those years ago. And, suddenly, it's all over. We've exchanged texts every night up until this week. I admit, they're just mundane texts about school stuff and family, never anything intimate, but still... .

I'd been hoping she'd break the silence first. That seems unlikely, now. I've got to be the one. I grab my cell phone and tap her smiling bright-eyed icon and start typing:

"Hi. How's it going?"

I press SEND. Wait. A moment later I see she's received my message: waving dots. I stare at them in anticipation, entranced. Finally, her response:

"Good!! You? GTGN. TTYL."

She sends along a smiley face emoji which absolutely crushes me more than ever. I'm left with no choice but to put all my cards on the table and send a bold, desperate question:

"Who's this new guy you're hanging out with?"

I take a deep breath, pause, and then press SEND. Moments pass. Waving dots. Ten seconds pass. Waving dots disappear. Come back. Go away again. I wait and wait but they never return. CODI goes off-line. A dagger rips out my heart.

Mom shouts from outside my room:

"Jordy, come out, please. Dinner is ready."

I mope out, turn and enter the dining room. I stop just inside the doorway. I see the guest. A paralyzing jolt of fear stops me dead. THE ASSHOLE - flashing a shit-eating grin - is sitting at the table, in my chair, next to dad.

Dad looks at me:

"Jordy, come in and sit down. Say hi to Snakes."

JORDY is MINE

28

Meanwhile, on her way out of the bathroom, Ariadne sees a butcher knife sitting in a knife holder on the kitchen counter. *That might come in handy.* She grabs it, hides it behind her back and returns to Sage's bedroom, stopping at the foot of the bed.

Sage is sitting up in bed smoking and reading *The National Enquirer.* She's pulled the blanket back over her lower body. She looks up at Ariadne.

"Where's Jordy?" laying the paper flat on her lap.

"Washing his hands. Where's Snakes?"

"Making a call."

"Jordy is mine and I'm not sharing him with you or anyone else."

Sage stabs out her cigarette in the bedside ashtray and picks up the highball. She gives Ariadne a hard look and takes a drink and sets the glass back down. She rests her hand down along her thigh, slowly inching it under the blanket till it finds a .38 revolver and wraps her fingers around it.

"You come into town with your flat chest and your horse

face and your dime store psychology but you're really nothing but a sexually frustrated two-bit social worker. Jordy's not interested in you," finishes off the highball, ice chinking, and sets the glass back on the nightstand. "Tell you what, come join the BROFOs and I'll get you laid - gang-bang style. Make you feel better."

"Thanks but no thanks. You can keep your money. I want out of our deal. I brought him home for you but he's got issues - Doreen and Tara issues - that I need to help him through."

"Ah, poor little Doreen. I helped him over that one. I bathed and comforted him, gave him my tit - the one he never got as a baby," angling the revolver up at Ariadne under the blanket, finger on its trigger.

"Where was it last spring when his dad died? It was being fondled by Snakes as the two of you plotted to rob him of his inheritance. And where was Jordy? He was languishing in a Minneapolis gutter. I took him in, cared for him, saved him from certain suicide with my therapy, got him to pursue his dream of being a screen writer, forged a new life for him as Johnny. I'm not letting you tear all that down," stepping forward, she sees the bulge under the blanket and brings out the knife. "I'm curious. Why did you divorce a good decent man like Jordy's dad. Jordy's had nothing but praise for him."

"Ha. He had Jordy brainwashed from the get go. He was a brute and a beast with a little limp dick." A slight smile curves her lips and a dreamy look comes into her eyes. "I dumped his ass when I met Snakes. He was having Jordy's dad make the special ink for printing the BROFO Bibles. We were living on the farm then. Snakes had come over to deliver a tub of methlamene for the ink. Later, he was cleaning up. I accidentally walked in on him in the shower. That's when I fell in love. I saw his horse meat. That sealed the deal," licking her lips, and smiling lustily, she moves her left hand down between her thighs. "Jordy's even bigger than Snakes. That's why you won't let him go."

Ariadne lunges at her with the knife.

Sage fires a shot and then another shot.

BENT PADDLE

29

Upstairs, Johnny's trip into Jordy's past is cut short upon hearing two gunshots. He slaps the journal shut and stuffs it back into the hole underneath the dresser. He pats around in the hole, wondering what other treasures may be hidden, when his hand lands on something cold and hard - a revolver.

"Sounds like your agent just bought the farm."

Johnny twists his head around to the direction of the voice - the closet in the corner behind him. The closet door swings all the way open and out stomps Snakes.

"You don't want her anyway," chomping on a slice of pizza. "Tara's your main squeeze." He devours the pizza up to the crust, tosses the rest on the floor, and steps into the room's doorway, blocking Johnny's exit should he be entertaining such thoughts. He reaches over and picks up the photo of Tara and looks at her. "Poor thing. This was her, last night. Have to admit, though, nice photography. Really captures her pain and suffering, don'tcha think," tossing it down into Johnny's lap. "Thanks go to Mongo for the rush job on developing and enlarging it. But don't worry. She's now safely in my brother BROFO's hands - no pun intended."

"If they've laid one finger on her," gripping the revolver tightly but keeping it hidden. "I'll personally castrate every last member and feed their nuts to the stray dogs out there on the street."

"Tut, tut, we are a Christian organization. Do you actually know why we're called the BROFOs? It's for Brother Fuckers. Do you know why we chose that name?"

"Beats me," shrugging. "You're a gay motorcycle club?"

"Asshole," slamming his wing-tipped Wellington boot into Johnny's thigh.

"Motherfucker!" Johnny falls forward against the dresser, wincing in pain.

"We're the Brother Fuckers because we ride for Jesus, praise His Holy Name. You blaspheme His Name? We fuck you up. Nobody fucks with the Brother Fuckers."

"I'll keep that in mind," massaging his sore thigh with his left hand.

"I was in the closet because that's where I go to pray. I heard the Lord speak to me. He told me Jordy needs saving from his life of sin. He abandoned his dying father last May. His dad had the virus. While Jordy was out stalking this hottie named Cody, he had his phone turned off. His pops couldn't reach him. So pops called me. I hopped on my hog and high tailed it out to the farm. Administered Last Rites on pour old pops. With his dying breath he gave me a message to pass on to his son. Barely able to breathe, he whispered, 'The bent paddle propels the way.' That mean anything to you?"

Johnny has heard those words somewhere before, but can't quite put his finger on it. "It's like one of those bent handled ergonomic shovels," he bluffs. "If you take a bent view of the world it's less strain on the brain."

"Don't fuck with me," bitch slapping Johnny. "It's a secret

code for where pops hid his last batch of Bible ink."

Johnny pulls the revolver out of the hole, stands and jabs it in Snakes' chest. "You stole Jordy's girl Cody. Then you dumped her so you could fuck his mom," his voice shaking. "Now you're going to die."

He fires the pistol.

Fffft-PLAPP.

A BB hits the flaming heart tattoo centered on Snakes' hairy chest. The BB ricochets off hid sternum and hits a wall.

"MOTHERFUCKER! That hurt," looking down at the nasty red welt on his chest. Then he starts laughing like a maniac. "You tried to kill me with a fucking BB gun? If you're gonna do a job. Do it right," pulling the .45 from his pants and holding to Johnny's forehead.

"You kill me and you'll never break that code."

"You got a valid point, punk. But I can make it very painful," lowering the revolver to Johnny's knee cap.

Remembering an old Christmas movie about a kid and a BB gun, Johnny raises his pistol and shoots Snakes directly in his right eye, hoping it has enough power give him a BB lobotomy.

Snakes drops the .45 and falls to his knees, hands covering his eye, screaming obscenities. Johnny shoves him over sideways with his foot, steps over him and out of the room, knocking over stacks of boxes behind him as he heads for the stairs.

Snakes fumbles for the .45, finds it and fires several wild shots through the doorway, missing Johnny as he flees down the stairs.

ESCAPE

30

Johnny stumbles down the stairs, his heart pounding. He falls against a stack of boxes in the living room and is grabbed from behind, a knife to his throat. He grabs the hand wielding the knife and wrenches it away, the knife falling on a mat of trampled newspapers.

"You're alive!" Ariadne says, hugging his head and kissing his forehead.

"You're alive," he says, no less happy. "Alright. Alright, enough kissing."

She helps him to his feet and they check each other over, relieved to find no bullet wounds.

"You're hands," he says, seeing them dripping with fresh blood.

"It's not mine. Hers," nodding her head toward the bedroom. "You know what?"

"What?"

"This was all worth it because, just now, for the first time, I think you actually felt something for me," hugging him. "I can't tell you how good that makes me feel."

"Don't jump to conclusions," peeling her off him. "Okay, I may *need* you, but *feel* is a bit too much." He pokes his head into Sage's electric-blue-flickering bedroom. "What happened in here?"

"She pulled a piece on me. I ducked and knifed her."

Sage is sprawled motionless soaked in blood. On the wall above her headboard, written in dripping blood - Mansonoid-style - is *PSYCHO BITCH.*

"Jesus."

"I had to make it witchy."

They both look up at the ceiling, hearing the thumping of Snakes' heavy footsteps and the crashing of boxes upstairs.

"We should blow," Johnny says, grabbing her hand and leading her out into the kitchen.

He sees Mongo's shotgun leaning against the wall by the back door and flashes back to that time in Goodman's house with Doreen.

"Our mission is to rid the world of psychos, is it not?" he says, grabbing the shotgun.

"It's our supreme Earthly goal," Ariadne says, thrilling at the sight of Johnny when he gets hard core.

"Upstairs, that biker dirt bag got so psycho, he was believing I was Rabnow and almost offed my ass. Time to eradicate Snakes," navigating his way back through the kitchen.

He can hear Snakes stopping down the stairs, shouting, "Ma, don't let that bastard get away."

Johnny cocks the hammer of the loaded barrel and waits at the stairs doorway, out of sight. He sees Snakes' wing-tipped Wellington boot land on the carpeted floor. His mangy-haired head pops into the dark living room, turned toward Sage's bedroom doorway, revolver raised in his right hand.Doesn't see Johnny at all.

BLAMMO!

Snakes flies and lands in the bedroom doorway amidst the piles of rubbish.

Johnny tosses the shotgun unto his convulsing body, turns, and makes his way back to Ariadne.

"When the Chinese find them, they'll see that cheese pizza and be so disgusted they'll call it murder-suicide."

Hanging on a coat rack hook by the back door he spots a ring of keys with a large cross on a keychain. He grabs it. They stumble through the dark back entranceway and make it out of the house.

Parked beside the junky garage is a chopper. Its coffin gas tank has *THE SAVIOR* painted across it in gothic. It's got ape hangers, a king-and-queen style seat, and a Honda 450 engine.

"C'mon," Johnny says. "Hop on."

They climb aboard. He finds the right key on the keyring and kicks the big hog, snorting and grunting, to life. He guns the throttle, blowing blue greasy exhaust out its ass end, shifts into first and peels out, pelting Sage's SUV with a spray of gravel. The loud obnoxious hog echoes across the yard as they fly out of the driveway.

Just down the block, Johnny hangs a right onto a dirt backroad that, a few miles up, runs past the Rabnow farm. He up-shifts and has the hog hitting 90 per. Ariadne hangs on for dear life - her arms wrapped tight around Johnny.

"What's the hurry," she shouts in his ear above the rushing wind.

"That fucker said the BROFOs have Tara. We need Jordy's help to save her."

RABNOW FARM

31

Two miles out of town Johnny lets off the throttle, down shifts, and turns onto a narrow tractor path running between two wheat fields. They follow it a third of a mile to a large grove of old elms, maples, cottonwoods, and ash trees - the outer edge of the Rabnow farm.

A full moon is up, casting eerie pale light.

Johnny idles the hog and lets it coast into the sparse trees on the edge of the grove. Shadows of long-abandoned farm implements haunt the woods. Through a gap in the trees they can see a glimpse of the farmyard.

He kills the engine. They sit and listen. All is quiet.

"We better park her here and walk in."

"Good thinking. Catch him napping," climbing off.

He dismounts after her and leans the bike against a stout elm. They start off towards the yard, moving slowly in the dim light, picking their way through the trees, having to maneuver around dead fallen branches and a graveyard of odd iron contraptions of days gone by.

They stop at the edge of the trees and scope out the yard.

The yard light lends the landscape the feel of the oppressive low intensity of a full solar eclipse.

The ramshackle house sits far off to their right, about a hundred yards away - no lights on. Across the yard from it, a hundred-year-old weathered barn leans on its deathbed. Dozens of smaller sheds and shacks of various shapes and sizes line the outskirts of the open yard. Overlooking it all, an old pioneer windmill creaks in the occasional lazy breeze (making Johnny feel like he's stepped into a scene from *Once Upon a Time in the West*). Distant frogs croak from the slough behind the house. Crickets chirp in the tall grass.

Dead ahead, a few hundred feet, they spot a car looking as out of place as an alien spaceship; a space-green KIA Soul.

"That's Tara's car," Johnny gasps. "She *is* here."

"Or, *has* been. He may have offed her already."

"Don't even think of it, c'mon. We better hurry and find her, who knows what Rabnow is up to."

They run out into the open yard, swishing through high barnyard grass, swerving around Canadian thistle patches, dodging man-sized cockle burs. The night air is sticky humid. By time they close-in on the car their clothes are sweat-damp.

The car sits ass-end to them, on the edge of a partially harvested wheat field. A hundred feet into the field hulks a huge rust-red Massey Harris Super 92 combine.

All is creepy quiet except for the chirping and the croaking and the creaking.

Johnny and Ariadne slow down, stop, and take a look around. No one in sight.

He looks harder at the car, glowing pale green in the oppressive moon. He sees the driver's door open in slow motion. A delicate sandal-clad red-toe-nailed foot emerges from the car and touches down into the shorter lush green grass. The door opens wider as long sexy legs pivot out. A woman's luxurious blonde head leans out, turns and smiles orgasmically into Johnny's eyes.

"TARA!"

He rushes up to her.

She stands, coming out of the car, and turns to him. She's totally nude. Her slender hips, dirty blonde bush, and perky breasts; all gleam vampiric in the green moonlight.

It suddenly all dawns on him. She's come to makeup.

The sweat is dripping from his face. His heart pounds in his throat.

Tara steps toward him, arms spread wide, her red lips parted for a soul kiss.

"Oh, baby," Johnny murmurs. "You don't know how this makes me feel," tasting her tongue in his mouth as he steps closer.

She mouthes something silent but he can't make it out because of the buzzing.

"You'll never fuck her," Ariadne says, behind him. To him it sounds like a voice from off-stage somewhere.

He feels a sharp slap on his cheek.

Tara vanishes.

"Nasty things are everywhere," Ariadne says, flicking a dead fly from Johnny's cheek.

"Thanks," he says, seeing them buzz around the car. "Think I had a momentary blackout."

Looking through the open driver's window, they see a couple dozen large black flies crawling on the dash and up the windshield.

"She wasn't alone," Johnny says, indicating two Starbucks cups in the console.

Potato chip bags, McDonalds burger cartons, a Chinese take-out container litter the floor. A couple bulging Nike duffle bags and an over-burdened North Face backpack take up the entire back seat.

"Looks like the passenger was of the Asian persuasion," he

says

"Bullhead?" Ariadne says, walking around to the front of the car. "Check this out."

Two lawn chairs, a cooler on the ground between them, sit in the short grass facing the field and the combine. She opens the cooler and plugs her nose; finding a couple six packs of beer, several cans of pop, steaks, and brats - all lounging in tepid water.

"A picnic waiting to happened."

"But never will."

One-by-one flies smell the rancid meat and congregate to the open cooler. Johnny kicks the lid shut.

"What happened here," Ariadne says, stepping away, swatting flies.

Looking around, Johnny points to the ass-end of the Super 92 combine, "They seem to be coming from over there."

The stubble ground behind the machine looks blanketed with a layer of spit-out straw and chaff. But there's something strange about that straw. Like it's been painted black. Walking over, Johnny steps in some of it. Pieces of painted straw stick to his shoes. He lifts his foot and picks off a piece, brings it up to his face.

"This shit's fucking blood."

The buzzing gets louder as flies swarm up. They swat in vain and move on. Walking along side the Super 92, it smells of grease, gas, and burnt pulley belts. At the combine's operator's platform ladder, a more gut wrenching odor hits - human decomp.

They cover their noses and, slowly, venture a few steps towards the combine's cutting head. Zillions of flies swarm up. And then they see it.

Johnny bends over and barfs in the wheat stubble. Ariadne freezes, fascinated, gawking like at a bad traffic accident. But this is way more intense.

The body of a man lies where the ripe wheat stalks normally enter the combine. The combine's spiked tooth pickup auger has mauled his head and shoulders to human hamburger.

"Was this an accident," Ariadne says. "Or is it a murder scene?"

"Looks like Rabnow killed again," Johnny says, wiping his mouth on his arm and stepping closer. "Before we could stop him. Judging from the vic's tight jeans, we've got ourselves a day-old bloater."

"Any theory on what happened?"

Johnny steps back to take-in the entire scene, framing it with his fingers to get a cinematic perspective. He gets a Will-Graham-esque vision, "All that bunched-up wheat grass laying on the ground behind the body must mean the combine was clogged. Rabnow was up in the control seat with his foot on the clutch when this poor bastard tried to unplug it. Rabnow's foot slips off the clutch pedal and, so long you poor fucker."

"How do we know that the vic here isn't Rabnow? You know, suicide by combine."

"Nah," shaking his head. "We know Tara arrived with a passenger. Probably showed up to help Rabnow with the harvest. Let's go up to the operator's platform," grabbing the ladder. "Might find some clues," after you.

Ariadne walks past the Combine's man-sized drive wheel and climbs up first and sits in the driver's seat. Johnny climbs up after her, stopping and standing on the ladder's top rung for lack of space, holding onto the guard rail.

"Look at the position of the control levers," he says, pointing to the panel of iron levers on her right. "The threshing lever is still engaged and the throttle is all the way up - the machine was going full-tilt-boogie. And the key is still on. It must have stalled when this poor fucker's skull went through. There's no way Jordy would leave the threshing mechanism engaged and jump down to unplug a jam. My theory is the passenger was Tara's boyfriend. Jordy had the guy go down around front, pull out the jammed straw, and then he let him have it - the perfect *accident* to do away with his rival."

"Sounds plausible. So, then what? Tara freaks? Jordy kidnaps her? Right now, does he have her over in the house over there," pointing over to the creepy looking dilapidated farmhouse back across the yard. "All cut up in pieces, or maybe, tied up in the cellar?"

They both look over at the dark house.

Ariadne's right foot steps on something lying on the platform floor between the seat and the control console. It's hard to see what it is in the dim moonlight. Could be a wrench or just a piece of rusty iron, but it's flat and it didn't feel *that* solid. She bends down for a closer look, finds the object and picks it up. A cell phone.

"Jordy's?"

"Will it open"

"Any guess at a passcode?"

"Psychos are so predictable. Try T-A-R-A."

Ariadne punches in the code and the phone comes alive. A check of its call log shows that Tara and her friend, Frankie Karpis, planned to drop in on Jordy and help with his harvest. That was two days ago. They check the phone's photo album and finds several stalker-quality pics of Tara. One shows an Asian dude whose shirt and jeans match those of the dead guy down in front of the combine. The latest file is a video taken two days ago.

"Play it," Johnny says. "Could be interesting."

"Sure you want to see it?"

"Go ahead."

Ariadne taps the file with her finger and the clip roles.

BLOODY HARVEST

32

Deafening grinding and growling noise. The view is from atop the combine's operator platform looking down as the machine gobbles up a thick swath of wheat heavily infested with cocker burs. Karpis is sitting in the drivers seat, steering the combine. It can be inferred that Jordy is standing beside him, giving instructions while shooting the video. He frequently pans down to a smiling bubbly Tara as she walks alongside the moving machine, watching and cheering encouragement to Karpis.

The combine lurches, choking on a large cockle bur. It's threshing mechanism jams. Loud screeching of stuck pulley belts.

"Quick, step on the clutch and release the threshing lever."

"This one?"

"Yeah, before the belt burns up."

Karpis steps on the clutch and pulls the iron lever up with considerable effort.

"Shit. We're fuckin' jammed. You gotta go down an pull out all that shit. FUCK! Shift into neutral. Yeah, like that. Now get down

there. We got a shit load a work to do."

Karpis climbs down the platform ladder and Jordy takes his place in the operator's seat.

Karpis walks around front of the combine and starts pulling wheat and weeds out of the header, sticking his arms and head way into its jaws.

Jordy pans his phone down to Tara watching off to the side about fifteen feet away. She offers Karpis words of encouragement and assurance that it's safe.

In the distance a couple hundred feet beyond Tara, somewhat out of focus, a woman appears out of the woods. But it's clear who she is. Ariadne. Even from that distance, her intense eyes penetrate the screen. She's looking straight at Jordy, flashing him some kind of weird occult hand signals.

The picture wobbles. Jordy is doing something off-screen with the control levers.

The threshing mechanism starts up.

Picture haphazardly flashes back to the front, capturing blood gushing up from the combine header.

Tara runs into the picture, hands covering her face, screaming hysterically.

The combine stalls. Screen blurs as the phone falls to the platform floor. Goes black.

WHO ARE YOU?

33

"Give me that," Johnny says, swiping the phone from her hands and pocketing it. He grabs her by the neck. "Who are you?"

"Johnny, don't. You don't want to go there."

He shoves her off the platform. She falls onto the wheat stubble, the wind knocked out of her. He climbs down, grabs a fistful of her hair and pulls her to her feet.

"Are you in league with Rabnow? Huh? What have you done with Tara? Tell me or I'll fucking feed you to that combine like Karpis there."

"Alright. Alright. Let's go
to the house. You'll see."

"Yeah, this better be good," grabbing her wrist and twisting it behind her back. He gives her a shove. "Start walking."

TWIN CITIES EXPOSED

34

Sitting beside each other in swivel chairs on the set of the late night talk show TWIN CITIES EXPOSED are Jordy Rabnow and Ravenna Huxley.

The talk show's host, Dirk Deschutes, is sitting to their left, angled slightly toward them, chain smoking cigarettes.

"Hi, everybody," Dirk says, all nonchalantly. "Welcome back. If you've just joined us, I'm talking with admitted sexual predator Jordy Rabnow and his therapist Ravenna Huxley," taking a drag off the cigarette ever present in his right hand. He leans back in his chair, lifts his right ankle up onto his left knee and exhales a long plume of blue smoke.

Jordy, a small table holding an ashtray and a couple water glasses between him and Dirk, sits upright and stiff, hands clasping his bouncing knees. He's very uptight to say the least.

Ravenna, sitting on the far side of Jordy (his left), casually has her left foot up on the seat of her chair, massaging her ankle, knees suggestively spread apart. She's turned-on about sharing her work to a late night TV audience.

"Jordy," Dirk continues. "You've admitted to being obsessed

with unattainable girls since, hell, you were a little squirt. And it's continued unabated to this day with your co-worker Tara. Tell me this, sir... Why? Look at yourself. You're a handsome guy. Hell, I'd even hit on you if I was of the right persuasion, ha-ha-ha. So, why can't you score?"

Ravenna looks expectantly at Jordy, sees his tongue-tied embarrassment and reaches over, squeezing his hand.

"I can answer that," she says. "He's a masochist."

"I think client-patient confidentiality just flew out the window," Dirk says, taking another drag and blowing smoke. "Ha-ha-ah."

"Tara only likes Asian guys," Jordy confesses. "She started [bleep] this Asian guy named Karpis."

"Ha-ha-ha. Easy on the language, guy. We're live."

"Sorry. It got me so bad I either had to kill the guy or run away as fas as possible. That's when Ravenna stepped in to help."

They exchange smiles.

"To help mitigate his anger," Ravenna explains, touching Jordy's hand. "I had him write down everything he was feeling."

"That fit in with my goal of being a writer. So I wrote down what I was going through and put it in screenplay format. Called it BULLHEAD... after the main character. Basically, I'm Bullhead - an Asian superhero who gets the girl, in the end," self-consciously lowering his eyes.

"How's that working out for you," Dirk says, tapping his cigarette on the ashtray and then taking another long drag.

"I can speak for that," Ravenna says. "It's helped ease some of Jordy's tension. But, when we attended Tara's birthday party last weekend, when she announced her engagement to Karpis, the rage reared its ugly head again. So we're planning on implementing a more robust brand of therapy."

"Example?"

"Hypnosis induced role playing. Together we're writing out a script where the entire country is taken over by China. Jordy plays a TV celebrity named Johnny Wonder. I play his agent, Ariadne.

Together we star in a reality show in which we hunt down and kill psychopaths."

"You think this will actually cure Jordy?"

"We hope it will enable him to adopt a stronger, healthier surrogate personality and kill off the possessive diseased one."

"Wish you both all the luck. Hey, we're almost out of time. One last question before we go. For your therapy to work you gotta get down and dirty with each other. Am I right?"

"Phew," Jordy shakes his head. "You don't want to know, believe me."

"Are you at all concerned about the two of you getting a bit too attached with each other?"

"I'd be a liar," Ravenna says, rubbing Jordy's knee and gazing lovingly at him. "If I din't admit to a little counter-transference. In fact, if this new therapy works, I wouldn't mind at all being stalked by this handsome devil."

WAKING Iin DARKNESS

35

Jordy Rabnow wakes.

He finds he's lying on his back in shallow water five or six inches deep. Water has intruded into his ears. His face is an island in this dark subterranean sea. He tries to open his eyes but his lashes seem to be glued together. He struggles to lift his left arm. Numb. Stiff.

How long have I been here?

After several attempts, he manages to touch his eyelids with his fingers. Covered with crusty muck. He sprinkles water on them and rubs them with his forefinger , slowly, the muck dissolves enough for him to pry open his eyes.

Inky darkness.

After awhile, he can make out vague shadows: card table, workbench, crude shelves loaded with large bottles, water pump, ceiling rafters, seven wood plank steps rising to a trapdoor.

Who closed it? Tara? Where is she?

The water level seems higher. The only sound is a slow steady dripping several feet away - leaky pipe on the pump.

He sniffs the air. Dank and foul like the inside of an inner tube, wet decaying concrete, and wet rusty iron. And something else, too. Underlying it all. Something more putrid. He's afraid of finding out just what the source of that gawd-awful stench might be.

He tries to move. *Gotta get up and get out.* Raises his head and lets the water drain out of his ears. A new, barely audible, sound sends a shiver rippling through his water-logged flesh.

A gurgling watery whisper, "Jordy… I… love… you… ."

"Huh, huh, who's there?" Jordy whispers through clattering teeth.

He tries hard to hear an answer but is overcome by a bout of the shakes.

Then a labored gasp disturbs the water a few feet away.

"Get help," says a voice from the grave.

He listens motionless for a long time but hears nothing.

He shrieks as a sudden frantic motion in the water moves straight for his head. Tiny claws scratch at his right cheek. He panics, thrashing in the water, trying to brush the creature away. It's small and furry with a leathery tail. It climbs up onto his face. He grabs it in his fist, its teeth biting his finger, pulls it off and flings it, making screeching noises. It splats against a wall and plops into the water.

He sinks back into the water, catching his breath.

The voice he'd heard came from off to his left. He reaches out his left arm and feels around, splashing water. His fingers graze something taught and rubbery. Inner tube? His fingers crawl up along the smooth thing's surface.

An arm.

"Hello?" he shudders.

No response. No movement.

He scoots over closer and feels small breasts.

"Ravenna?"

He struggles to sit up and twists over and shakes the

body's shoulders. Stiff as a corpse. He lowers his cheek to her lips. Nothing. Pinches his nostrils against the putrid stench.

He rises to one knee and then tries to stand but a painful Charlie horse pulls him down on his ass. He grabs his leg and works it out.

After awhile he gains his feet and hobbles over to the plank steps that lead up to the trapdoor that opens up into the farmhouse bathroom. He suddenly realizes he's back on the farm. Back home. Thank God.

Memories.

He slowly lowers himself down onto the second step and lets his face fall into his hands.

"What have I done," sobbing. "Tara, what are we going to do?"

We could hide out here. Away from everyone. Could live together and work the farm. Live off the land. Just like grandpa did in the old days. How life was meant to be lived. No pain-in-the-asses telling you what to do. No government meddling. Dad would be very happy that he was carrying on the family farm. Yes.

Jordy lifts his head, leans back, takes a long deep breath and slowly lets it out, closing his eyes. He sees dad, back in the golden days when he was stout and strong and everything was good. He can even hear his voice.

FARM MEMORIES

36

It was on the farm that I fell under the terrible spell of sexual obsession. At the age of twelve I first experienced the infinite bliss that close contact with a girl could bring and that, it and it alone, was the sum total and end of all earthly existence.

The farm is a 40 acre plot of land two miles from town. And, for practical purposes, totally isolated from almost all humanity. The yard, with its huge wrap-around tree grove and many sheds and the rushing Doran slough, offered ample opportunities for adventure. But most of my time was occupied with the drudgery and boredom of farm work: tilling, planting, combining, plowing (took a great chunk out of my TV time). While slaving away, I dreamed of being a filmmaker.

But the farm had been in the family since 1878. Dad had plans of one-day handing it down to me. To make ends meet, he taught high school science and also operated a custom woodworking business out of the farm wood shop. I helped him with that. Actually enjoyed it. At least it offered an outlet for my creative juices.

I was lonely. We got few visitors: neighboring farmers, woodworking customers, an aunt and uncle. They'd stop by with my cousin, Doreen. While her parents tended their garden plot, me and Doreen would run off and explore the woods or something. Doreen made me feel alive. We had fun... until that fateful harvest of my thirteenth year... And that horrible stain.

Everyone saw the stain. Stigmatized me for the rest of my school days. After the combine incident I saw Doreen one more time... alive. And, in the ensuing months and years, many more times, as she is preserved for all eternity. She became my almost constant spiritual companion, as I would commune with her, have conversations with her. One might even go so far as to say I prayed to her at times when I felt lonely or down in the dumps about something - and she would be present, cheer me up, make me feel less alone.

Throughout my teens I isolated myself as in a cave - farming, woodworking, TV, and loosing myself in dreams of getting away and going to film school.

Last spring dad got the dreaded virus. It was a short one-month struggle that ended leaving me all by myself on the farm (mom divorced him earlier in the winter - I believe the trauma of that ordeal made him vulnerable, weakened him). But, for the first time in my life, I felt totally free. I said, "damn the crops." Packed my bags and hit the high road for the artist's life in Minneapolis.

MEETING RAVENNA

37

I blow into Minneapolis in late May with nothing but my typewriter, a portable DVD player, a bag of books and DVDs, and the clothes on my back. The guy at the Y says I have to wait a few days for my room to be sanitized. I bum around Hennepin Avenue - dog tired - and come upon an art gallery showing Hitchcock's *Vertigo*.

Go in. Grab a seat. Film ends. Lights come on. People get up. Start chatting in little cliques.

Lots of hot young babes. I get up to check out the surrealist art on the walls when I feel my left ass cheek grabbed and squeezed. Turn and find myself face-to-face with a tall horse-faced woman a few years older than me with a Cleopatra haircut and no tits.

"Hello, handsome," Horse-face says in a husky voice. "New in town?"

Her thin red lips curve up in a rye smile. Her narrow grey eyes leer out from under long black lashes and electric blue eye shadow. She holds a rakish pose, her lanky frame glittering in a sleeveless mid-thigh midnight-blue sequined gown. Her fishnet-covered knee knocks my crusty denim covered knee.

"Guess you could say that," stepping back, pulling my ass away from her hand. "Interesting art here."

I turn and move toward the nearest wall, relieved she doesn't follow. Spot a lone hot blonde and work my way casually over.

"So, you an artist, yourself?"

I turn and find horse-face is back, holding two glasses of wine. She holds one out. I take it because I sure could use a drink.

"Because, if you are, you're in the right place," clinking my plastic wine glass. "To art," taking a sip.

I gulp mine. Feels good going down. Warms me and loosens me.

"More of a writer," nodding toward my vintage typewriter case still sitting on the floor over by my folding chair. She follows my gaze. Her eyes pop. I take another swallow of wine.

"Shit. You're old school. Hardboiled. Fuck. I love that shit," shifting her body around so that we're standing side-by-side, hip-to-hip, admiring the typewriter case. "What kind of stuff you write?" subtly slipping her free left hand around my waist, just above the rivet belt holding up my travel-worn Levis. I'm not used to these bold big-city women and I'm not quite sure how to respond to her aggressiveness without being rude so I let it slide, for now.

I ignore the come-on, more interested in finally getting the opportunity to talk about my writing. "I'm working on a teleplay for a TV show."

"No shit! I'm a film student. Ravenna Huxley," taking her hand off my waist so she can transfer her wine glass into it. She grabs my hand and shakes it.

"Jordy Rabnow," I say, her long bony fingers digging into

me claw-like.

"So," smiling excitedly while shifting the wine glass back into her right and casually replacing her left hand back loosely around my waist as if staking her claim on me. "Tell me about your teleplay."

"Well," looking down at my shoes, a bit tongue-tied because I haven't worked out how to really explain it yet. "It's kind a pop-ish. You'll probably think it's stupid and juvenile," looking up at her and shrugging with a nervous little half-smile.

"Try me," biting her lower lip and tilting her head to one side. She gives me a puppy dog look, pulling me in ever so slightly - enough to feel her vibes and smell her scent; fresh as honeysuckle in heat.

"Okay, I give in. But don't say I didn't warn you... it's called *Bullhead*. About this nerdy guy - a cubicle drone at FBI Headquarters. He's hot for this blonde field agent. Whenever she gets into trouble with the bad guys he transforms into a giant black catfish with razor-sharp fins, bullet-proof scales, and poisonous stingers on his ugly head. He kicks ass on the bad guys and wins the blonde."

"That sounds so corny," laughing so hard that she spits up wine. "That people might actually go for it. Excuse me," wiping her lips with a tissue from her tiny purse. "I didn't mean to make fun. I'd actually like you to read it to me. Got friends in Hollywood that worked on some shows. They got connections. Could get it produced for you," nodding her head encouragingly.

She turns into me, hooking a stiletto foot behind my left knee, pulling me in tight. She gazes deep into my eyes. "We'll make a good team," her wine breath hot on my lips. "Kiss me."

She's put me in a tight spot. Not knowing what else to do, I touch her lips softly with mine and am about to pull away when she wraps an arm around my neck and forces her tongue into my mouth. I go with it. Actually feels good. Then I push her off.

"Thanks for the offer," taking a step back. She drops her hands at her sides, lets her shoulders droop and feigns a pout. "But... it's not done yet."

"Need a place to stay? To work on it? You can crash at my place."

"No thanks," slowly moving away. "Got a room being sanitized for me at the Y," gulping down the last of my wine and leaving the glass on the bar.

"Ugh," grimacing. "Don't go there... Well, you'll need a place to stay till then, yes?"

She intercepts me on my way to get my typewriter and bags. I dodge her gaze and shrug off her grasping hand.

"At least give me your number."

"Sorry, it's been nice meeting you but I don't need your help," picking up my things. I thread my way through the chattering crowd. I can sense her eyes follow me to the door. I don't look back, relieved to be back out on Hennepin in the crisp invigorating city night air.

HOOKED ON TARA

38

Leaving the art gallery I walk up and down streets, looking for a lonely hidden spot to spend the night. I get jumped and mugged. Mysteriously, I wakeup late the next day in Ravenna's apartment. She says she followed me. I don't know if I can believe her but she does have a cool loft in the Warehouse District.

She works out a deal with me where I can stay in her spare bedroom rent-free in exchange for sex. I know, right? Hard to believe a girl doing that. But it's weird ritualistic sex involving a lot of chanting, symbolism, and religious robes. Maybe even satanic, who knows. But I say, "Okay," not expecting her to demand it every night. She's completely repulsive. I've got to get out before she starts drinking my blood or draining my soul.

Within days I land a temp job with Fulfillment Services doing assembly work. It's a soul-sucking job - making boxes all day, everyday. Other workers fill the boxes with dietary supplements or sex toys or some such crap and ship the stuff out all over the country.

The only bright spot is getting to work along side a hot blonde named Tara. She could be Doreen's twin - Doreen at twenty-two. Can barely keep my eyes off her. The bitch boss lady keeps telling me to "pick up the pace."

The production line is done by noon. After that, I'm stuck at the bagging table while Tara comes and goes as she pleases - taking extra cigarette breaks or buzzing off to the coffee shop for more ice coffee. She keeps the cup on her push cart as she goes around the warehouse picking product to fulfill special orders. Even when she's way off on the other side of the stacks, I can hear her infectious laughter.

Doreen has been reincarnated. I can reclaim my lost love.

Even though I don't smoke, I go out and bum a smoke off Tara. I'm in luck. She's alone, sitting on the small wooden bench out behind the building with a great view of the employee parking lot. She's playing with her phone.

"Got an extra smoke," I quietly say, walking over to her.

"Didn't know you smoked?" digging out a cig from the pack beside her on the bench.

"Just now and then," taking it from her and sitting down beside her. She hands me her lighter and I light up, handing back the lighter. I puff but don't inhale. She goes on playing with her phone. "So, seeing anyone?" casually looking over at her, raising my eyebrows.

She looks up from her phone and gives me the most heart-melting smile. "Not exactly." Then the most merry laugh bursts from her lips. "Wanna ask me out?"

My jaw hits the asphalt and little bursts of subatomic explosions batter my chest cavity. "Duh, ye-ah. Who wouldn't." My fingers are trembling and I'm afraid of dropping the cigarette so I hold it away where she can't see it.

"Sorry, stud. You're sweet and good looking but... ," gives me a lost puppy look. "I only like Asian guys. Sorry."

I reel in my tongue and retract my jaw. "No, no. That's okay… well, will you at least have coffee with me sometime, just as friends? I found this great bagel shop that I've been dying to try out. It's on Lake Street near Lake Calhoun ."

"Mmm… I think I know the place. Just opened. *Hobiton Bagel Co.*, right?"

"Yeah, that's it! Wanna check it out? Sounds fun."

"You hit me in my weak spot, coffee… okay. You're on. What do you say, Saturday morning? About nine-ish?"

"Great! I'll be there."

I fly high all week only to be stood-up. Puts my mood in the shitter. But, for some reason, I want her now more than ever.

To escape the emotional pain of rejection, I bring a copy of *Woodworking Enthusiast* to work and leaf through it during my breaks. Takes me back to more carefree times in dad's wood shop.

I'm sitting at one of the plastic picnic tables in the break room when Tara comes in and sits down beside me, coffee in hand.

"Whatcha looking at, handsome?"

"Oh, just stuff people made out of wood," not looking up from the magazine because I'm walking a treacherous line between repulsion and desire and the tension is making a wreck out of me. I take a sip of my own coffee and flip the page.

"Hey, that one's way cool," leaning an elbow on my shoulder and planting a slender nail-polished finger on the picture and drawing the mag a little closer to herself.

Her left breast ever-so-slightly grazes my right upper arm (think of it, there was just one thin layer of work t-shirt cotton and a layer of bra fabric between me and paradise). I am completely engulfed in the effluvium of her bodily fragrance

(like a kind of citrusy-sea breeze that literally takes my breath away). I'm lost for a moment and then come back to earth when I realize she's talking to me. I have a sudden hard-on and am doubly thankful; one, that I didn't cum in my pants (creating another *stain* episode) and two, that the picnic table top is able to hide it (hoping it'll subside before break is over).

"I like how it's, like, artsy," she says, referring to a picture of a cabinet in the mag. "Slender and curvy, elegant and light hearted. Like something out of a Dr. Seus book."

"Yeah," taking a deep breath and hoping she doesn't notice my profuse sweating. "I don't know how the guy made it, but I bet I could figure it out."

"OMG, Jordy," clutching my wrist. "Serious? You could make this? Get out of here," shoving my shoulder. She sees I'm dead serious. "You really can, can't you?"

I smile, nodding vigorously.

"I didn't know you were a woodworker."

"Shoot yeah," both knees bouncing with building erotic energy. "Got a fully stocked shop back on the farm."

"You really think you could build this for me?"

"Course I can. Just need the dimensions. How big you want it?"

"Not sure. There's an empty spot in my bedroom where it'd be perfect."

"I'll need exact measurements," taking a sip of coffee to try and relax.

"Can you come by with a yardstick?"

"This Saturday," barely able to squeak out the words because I'm not believing my luck. I take another sip. "Would early afternoon work?"

"Hmmm?" tapping a finger against her forehead. "I was gonna go to the mall... but that can wait. Shall we say one-ish?"

"Perfect."

"Here's my address and number," scribbling it on a napkin. She then takes out her phone. "I'm putting this on my calendar. No screw-ups this time." Our knees touch as she types. I can feel her body heat (she's just as excited about this as I am!). "Great! Can't wait. Thanks, hun," squeezing my shoulders briefly as she grabs her coffee and gets up. "Gotta go have a quick smoke before break's up… want one, too?"

"Ah, no, no, I'm good, thanks."

KARPIS STARTS AS A TEMP

39

The next day at work we get a new temp. Asian guy by the name of Frankie Karpis. He and Tara seem to enjoy working together a little too much. Concerns me.

ROUGH SKETCH

40

Saturday, Tara brings me up into her bedroom to take measurements for the cabinet. That done, we sit at her kitchen table and sip coffee while I do a rough sketch of the cabinet.

"This is going to be fucking awesome, Jordy."

I smell her sweet mocha breath and watch her juicy pink tongue as she mouthes the words. It's all in close-up and slow motion. I picture her tongue inside my mouth, entwined with mine.

Heavy breathing.

She's doing this on purpose. Wants it as bad as I do. It will happen today. In her bed. Before the day is done we'll be boyfriend and girlfriend.

My eyes crawl out of her mouth and climb over the lush landscape of her lips, and creep over to her downy cheek with its smattering of pimples (her only imperfection). They only intensify my desire. I would lay down my life just for the chance to suck their sebum.

I lean forward for a kiss.

Her phone alarm goes off.

"Oops. Sorry, Jordy," getting up. "I have to do something."

She goes into the bathroom and returns with a packet of birth control pills.

What's this!!!?

Seeing them makes me tremble with fear. Is she already fucking Karpis? She's only known him a couple days.

"Will you do me a favor, hun? Read the instructions to me?" pulling them out of the box and holding them out to me. "Wanna make sure I get the times right and everything."

Sweat beads my forehead. My fingers tremble as I shake the little piece of paper to unfold its many folds and try to read the tiny writing. My throat is a dry rusty-hinge. The words come out as low squeaks.

Unbearable torture.

"Why," my shaky voice cracking. I try to work-up a little saliva and swallow. "Why are you taking these?" afraid of the answer, but I need to hear it.

"My doctor prescribed them for my acne, silly," slapping my shoulder and studying me. She bursts out laughing. "You thought I was fooling around, didn't you? Relax. The acne," pointing to her cheeks.

Sure enough, I see "treatment for acne" listed on the instructions. A ten ton weight falls from my heart. I'm flying high again. The cabinet is the key to her heart. So long, Karpis, you sucker.

ROLLERCOASTER

41

Everyday at work I ride a rollercoaster between the hills of erotic enticement and the pits of seething jealousy. Complicating matters, at home, Ravenna is becoming increasingly irritable because I've been cutting off her sexual demands. She makes me sleep with my door open. At times I have to physically fight her off.

I relish the chance to get away on weekends - calling in sick on Fridays or Mondays so I can have a three-day-weekend - to be alone on the old homestead and lose myself in building Tara's cabinet.

It's carried me like a life preserver through a sweltering summer of unfulfilled desire. But, I'm almost done, bringing a new dawn of hope. Tara will soon be mine.

HARRASSMENT

42

Monday, back at work. My most traumatic day yet. So much so I can't work. I have to bypass that bitch supervisor and go straight to the manager.

"What can I do for you, Jordy?" he says as I step into his small office just off the production floor. "You don't look well. Come in. Close the door and have a seat."

"Something's bothering me," licking my dry lips. Sitting down helps take some of the stress off my palpitating heart. The best way to unburden my load is to be blunt right up front. "I've been observing a pattern of explicit sexual... ah, teasing, going on between this new temp, Karpis, and Tara."

"Oh?" frowning from behind his desk. He sets down his doughnut mid-bite and leans forward on his elbows. "What exactly has been going on?"

"Ah," my voice trembling. "Lewd language... sexually suggestive gestures... . Once I saw him, ah, dry hump Tara in the stacks. And, this morning, when he asked her to bring him a doughnut, she said, 'Want a glazed one?' 'One with a hole in it,' he said, back to her from across the bay. To which she replied, 'I'll give you a hole.' 'And I'll pound it, too,' he shouted back. Then, they both laughed. It's direct sexual harassment. I'm so stressed out by it I can't work. If it doesn't stop I'll have to quit."

"No, no, Jordy. I don't want you to do that. You're a fine worker and we all like you. You're right. You shouldn't have to put up with that kind of behavior. This is what I'm going to do. I'll call them each into my office separately and warn them that this sort of thing will not be tolerated. And, if it goes on, Karpis will be gone and Tara will be reprimanded."

"Thank you, sir," letting out a deep breath.

"Is there anything else I can do for you, Jordy?"

"No, sir. Thank you. I feel a lot better, now," getting up. I walk over to the door and open it. He gets up, walks around his desk, and follows me out.

"Thank you for bringing this to my attention, Jordy," stopping at the door. "Keep up the good work."

I return to the production area, getting questioning stares from everyone, but I keep to myself, a glimmer of a smile in my heart and feeling much relieved and hopeful.

DELIVERING the CABINET

43

Weeks go by.

Woodworking offers me solace.

I finish the cabinet, load it onto the old 1949 GMC farm pickup and haul ass back to the Cities, straight to Tara's house. Run up her side steps and give her door a tap. She looks out the window and comes to the door.

"Jordy! What are you... ."

Through the open door I see Karpis seated at the kitchen table (same chair I sat in to draw up the plans for the cabinet just a few weeks ago). Tara sees the fear and anger contort my face. She pulls me inside and shuts the door. Karpis turns his head, sees me, scared look comes over his face. He pushes out his chair and stands.

I stand, middle of the kitchen, fists clenched at my sides, about ready to punch the living daylights out of that Asian bastard.

"Okay," Tara says, a dynamo of righteous energy. "You two are going to shake hands and be friends or I'll never speak to either of you ever again."

Karpis bows at the waist, offering his hand, "My humble apologies for any offense, Mr. Rabnow."

I snarl, look over at Tara standing with her hands on her hips and the most adorable angry kitten look on her face. Seeing it, I almost cream my pants.

"No problem, I guess," slapping my hand into Karpis' scrawny little thing. Give it a token shake and swat it away. I wipe my hand on my jeans and smile up at Tara. "Got the cabinet done. Wanted to bring it right over."

"Fucking awesome," jumping up and down and hugging me. "Frankie, you gotta see what Jordy made me." Turning to me, "Is it outside?" She rushes to the door, opens it and looks out at the pickup backed up behind her KIA Soul in the drive. "Ohhh, there it is. I see it!" almost peeing herself. She turns back to me, I've walked up behind her, and then shoots a quick glance back at Karpis by the table. "Jordy, I was just helping Frankie with his ESL lesson. We're almost done. Just take a few more minutes," biting her lower lip. "Mind?"

"Sure, go ahead. I'm thirsty from the long drive. Got anything in the fridge?"

"Oh, yeah, help yourself to anything."

She and Karpis sit back down and finish their lesson. I grab a beer while I wait, watching them fawn over each other. My anger seethes.

A little bit later, Karpis helps me carry the cabinet up to Tara's bedroom. I position it in the dormer - facing her bed. She is ecstatic. Gives me a big hug and a kiss on the cheek.

I don't hang around - telling her I'm extremely tired from the drive. I race home, hoping Ravenna isn't there (need to log-on to the webcam I hid inside the cabinet's top drawer).

EXPLICIT WEBCAM

44

In my bedroom , I get undressed, hop into bed and open the webcam's live feed window on my laptop.

"FUCK... FUCK FUCK FUCK FUCK!"

My calculations were slightly off. Instead of a view of Tara's bed, I get a shot of the wall behind it. At least it's audio is working.

"Get the K.Y. Jelly, dear," Tara says.

"Where is it?" Karpis says.

"FUCK! That asshole is still with her."

My heart starts banging like a chest full of firecrackers.

"Top drawer of Jordy's cabinet," Tara says.

A small erect penis with tufts of jet black pubes comes into view. Gets closer, and closer, until it's in my face. It takes all the restraint I can muster to keep from punching the laptop screen. Karpis opens the top drawer of the cabinet.

"For a looser," Karpis laughs. "Your friend makes a good cabinet."

"Ohhh, you're dead meat, fucker," shouting at my laptop.

"Jordy's a sweet guy. Bring the lube and come to bed,

lover."

Karpis leaves the drawer open and I see his tiny ass scurry back to the bed.

The extended drawer lowers the cam's sight angle just enough to give me the view I've dreamed of - Tara nude. She's laying on her back, legs partially spread, smiling like a sucubus. Karpis climbs into bed and mounts her. They kiss. She helps him in and he begins thrusting - slowly and rhythmically.

I bury my head under my pillow. But, after a few seconds, I can't resist another look. I hate it but I can't tear myself away now, getting a strange vicarious feeling of finally having her through the strange mutant medium of Karpis' loathsome body. I'm erect and start pleasuring myself.

"What are you watching?" Ravenna says, suddenly appearing in my bedroom doorway. She comes over and sits on the edge of my bed, leaning over to see my laptop's screen. I ignore her and continue masturbating.

"Wait," Ravenna's voice angry. "Is that that slut from your work? It is. What did you do, you devious bastard? Plant a cam on her? Oh, you incorrigible perv," grabbing my balls and squeezing tight. "These belong to me, mister," reaching over with her other hand and slamming the laptop shut.

I frantically re-open it and re-connect the feed. Ravenna's fighting me all the time. She knocks the laptop off the bed.

"You help me kill that bastard," furious and frustrated. "And you can play with me all you like."

"Deal, big boy," tearing her jeans off and pinning me down.

I let her mercilessly rape me over and over throughout the night. I feel I died that night. Died and languished in hell. My only way out was to be reborn as somebody else.

FINISHING the SCREENPLAY

45

Chop… chop… chop… .

The eerie slo-mo heart beat of the TV show pulses from my 72" flatscreen perched atop my cheap thrift store dresser. Tall jungle palms fill the screen. Something dark and scaly flashes by, fins-a-blur, buzzing like chopper blades, trailing contrails of blood. The camera pulls back revealing a dismembered corpse and automobile wreckage spewing black smoke - incense of the apocalypse.

I feel the world is coming to an end.

Knock. Knock. Knock.

I've lain here naked for days - subsisting on beer, sunflower seeds, beef jerky, and cable TV (binging on Batman and Project Runway). Dog-eared superhero comics litter my bed and spill-over onto the dusty hardwood floor. The fake-wood paneled walls are plastered with my lists and ideas about characters for my screenplay. I got a huge white dry-erase board hanging on one wall - covered with multi-colored spaghetti diagrams of plot scenarios and backstories. If you walked in on me right now you might think I'm tracking a serial killer. Nope, just writing a screenplay.

POUND. POUND. POUND.

"Open up, Jordy," Ravenna says, outside my door, rattling the door knob. "I thought I made it clear. This door is never to be closed."

"You only meant that metaphorically," I shout from my bed, hugging my soiled pillow.

I roll over, out of a pool of sweat, reach down into my bedside cooler and pull out a dripping Hamms pounder. I pop it, spraying foam on my hairless pale chest, and guzzle a quarter of the can. Clears my mind. Have no clue what time it is. Get up naked. Miserable sticky flesh. Look out the window. Sun-drenched street makes me squint. People float by. Swish of traffic.

KICK! KICK! KICK!

"You can't stay in there forever," Ravenna says, a little more subdued. "Let me in. I just want to talk."

Drain the rest of my Hamms and toss the empty at the over-flowing waste basket in the corner. It bounces off and jangles on the floor. I pad over and unlock the door.

"C'mon in," turning and heading back to my bed.

"Jesus, did something die in here? Open a window," waving her hand in front of her face as she goes over and lifts the window. She sees the orange juice jug half full of piss sitting on the closet floor. "Jordy, you got issues."

"Doesn't everyone?" I grab two beers out of the cooler. "Want one?" holding one to her.

"Ugg, how can you drink piss water?" She takes the can anyway, pops it, and clanks it to mine. "Cheers." She takes a swallow and sits in the chair at my writing desk, glances over at the sheet stuck in my typewriter. "How's the *Bullhead* screenplay coming?"

"You're looking at the last page. Just need the final line," taking a swig and leaning back in bed.

"That's fantastic," getting up, coming over and sitting on the bed. She pats my inner thigh and flashes me a crooked smile. "Let me proof read it… . By the way, your boss called again."

"Fuck. Told you not to pick up for that guy," rolling over on my side, away from her.

"Jordy, you haven't worked in a week. I need some money for rent."

"I'll never go back to that hell hole."

"Either you go back or I'm cutting the cable TV."

"Don't you dare pull that shit," looking over at the flatscreen TV. Project Runway is on. The judges are wowing over the creation of a designer named Wong. I've followed Wong through each episode, getting inspiration for my screenplay. "Don't do it. Not yet. I need to see if this guy wins. That's how I'm going to get my last line."

"Well, then you'll either have to give me some more sugar," grabbing my hip, pulling me back toward her, smiling tentatively. "Or give me some rent money."

I look at her overly-made-up horse-face and feel the need to barf.

"Let me think about it."

"Now," lifting her eyebrows. "Now, or I call and cancel the cable, right now."

Can't suffer another minute of Fulfillment Solutions.

"Okay, okay, make it quick."

I turn my face away as she blows me. Reach over, open my

laptop, and log onto the Tara cam. Been days since I bothered viewing it. I scroll back through its memory to see what Tara and Karpis were up to last night. It's repulsing, but at least it takes my mind off Ravenna. Tara and Karpis are engaged in what seems like post-coital chat.

"You know, Ding, my love," Tara says, her mussed blonde head resting on his olive-toned chest. "We can't keep this up forever. Someone is going to find you out - you're illegal status and your real name."

Can't believe my ears. My heart bursts with new hope. Ravenna thinks my excitement is for her, disrobing and mounting me. I push her off.

"What are you doing?" She says, her flailing hands fighting me.

"Get off me. Get out. I'm going back to work, tomorrow."

I WANT HIM GONE

46

Monday at work, immediately after morning break, Maxine Zender, the HR director, calls me up to her office. She's likable but can't be trusted - has a permanent smile pasted on her face.

I tap on her door.

"Oh, Jordy," looking up from her computer. She stands, smiling. "Come in. Please, have a seat."

Wondering what's up, I go in. The office is small and claustrophobic. I sit in one of the two Prison Industries chairs facing her desk.

"Welcome back. How are you," she says, as genuine as a spider on a wedding cake.

"Oh, ah, doing a little better, I guess," my right arm folded across my chest, palm cupping my left elbow, and my chin resting in the crook between my left thumb and forefinger - this way she can read less of my facial expressions. "But still have some anxiety over that thing with the Asian guy and Tara."

"Well, I can assure you that it has been addressed and it

shouldn't happen again." She clears her throat, shifts in her chair, glances briefly at an open folder laying on her desk and then looks back up at me. My eyes are wandering around the room, mainly on the cruddy orange carpet. "I understand you built a very nice cabinet for Tara."

"Yeah," nodding in my hand but dodging her piercing gaze to critique the framed pic of her family of porkers sitting on her desk at an angle. Like an asshole she pauses, waiting for me to elaborate. "It was something she wanted weeks ago. Made it in my dad's shop," unfolding my arms and wiping my sweaty palms on my jeans. Where is this leading?

"You're a very gifted man." She lets out a sigh and my darting glance sees her smile has flatlined. "Jordy, Tara found a webcam hidden inside the cabinet," opening a desk drawer, she reaches in and takes out the small video cam, placing it on top of the desk.

My heart stops and my lips go dry. I lick them, "Ahh, that's not mine," unable to control my shaky voice.

"This is very serious, Jordy. You could be in a lot of trouble."

"This is bullshit," leaning forward. "That Chinese guy is trying to get back at me and frame me."

"Let me tell you what could happen," leaning forward with her elbows on her desk, her fingers interlaced. "You could go to prison and be labeled a sex offender for the rest of your life... unless, you let us help you," leaning back in her squeaky desk chair.

"Us?"

"Yes. Tara has agreed not to press charges. She likes you and wants to see you get over this, as do we all here at Fulfillment Services. Let us help you, Jordy."

"Help me how?"

"This week I've had some good conversations with your roommate, Ravenna. She called in sick for you everyday."

That fucking bitch.

"You're lucky to have her. She explained about the screenplay you've been writing, that you just had to, 'git-er-done.' Anyway, this morning, after Tara had told me about the webcam, I called Ravenna..."

Meddling fucking bitch!

"... and apprised her of the situation. She wants to personally help you work through this, get you back on your 'emotional feet,' is how she put it. She promised me that she would personally see that you get sexual addiction counseling."

Yeah, right. Like she needs it more than I do.

After a long tense pause, "Is this something you'd agree to, Jordy?"

"If... ," looking boldly in the eyes. "If I agree to go along with this... this therapy, then I won't get into trouble?"

"You have my word and Tara has agreed, also. You can come back to work and there'll be no need of any documentation of the webcam incident."

"Can I get that in writing?"

"What I will do is make a note of our agreement in your file, which is strictly confidential."

"Well, I'm not going to agree," my voice taking an angry tone. "I have a condition of my own."

"Oh?" shocked look on her face.

"Yes. I have proof the Frankie Karpis is an illegal immigrant. His real name is Ding something. Got him admitting it on video. In fact, that is the real reason I planted the cam. I had my suspicions and wanted to nail him. I want him terminated and turned over to immigration officials."

"That's a very serious charge. I'll need that video file."

"I'll email a copy of it to you. I want him gone by the end of the week," getting up.

"If what you say is true, he will be," standing up also.

"Believe me, we do not tolerate illegal hiring practices here... . Jordy, you look pale. Are you alright?"

"I think I need to go home and relax. This has all been way too stressful."

DEATH or EXHILE

47

The following Friday Tara's friends throw a birthday party for her at a downtown grunge bar called *The Stratford*. Ravenna comes along to make sure I stay out of trouble. Tara is the life of the party; surrounded by friends, and, of course, Karpis.

Shit!

"Let's grab a booth," I say to Ravenna as we walk in. "Can't believe that asshole is still in town."

My stomach tightens, my lungs constrict. I take slow deep breathes.

The barmaid comes by. I get a Hamms, Ravenna orders a brandy Manhattan.

"You alright, sweetie?" Ravenna says, touching my hand. "My god, you're cold and sweaty."

"This greasy air is making me nauseous," sliding out of the booth. "I'm going to find the john," heading towards the back of the long narrow bar.

"Hey, Jordy," Tara shouts, flashing her perfect smile and wiggling her fingers at me. I stop next to her. "Thanks for coming," giving me a token hug. She's already half drunk.

"Wouldn't miss it. Happy birthday. Ah, would you excuse me? Have to use the restroom really bad."

"Okay, talk to you later."

Karpis greets me but I ignore him and continue down the long narrow hall past the swinging kitchen door. The men's room looks like a toxic waste dump. I yank the light string and a fly-speckled sixty watt bare bulb glows.

I can't take this. What does it take to get rid of that fucker?

Suddenly, without reason, my pulse jumps.

I look in the blurry mirror and see my face is pale as a corpse. Yet I'm burning up. I run some cold water in the sink and splash some on my scruffy face. I look back up at myself. I look like shit.

You're alright. You're alright. You're alright. You are Jordy Rabnow. You'll get through this.

I try to smile but it comes out weak and twisted. The room gets fuzzy, grainy dark. I can't go back out there. But, if I stay in here too long Ravenna will come looking.

Fuck it.

Stiff-arming the wall for support, I slog over into the dark shadowy stall.

I notice a pin-point of light coming from behind the toilet. Feebly, I squat down for a closer look. The light is coming from a pencil-thin hole some pervert had burrowed through the wall to peep into the lady's room. I put my eye right up to the hole.

Fuck me, I see Karpis.

What the fuck?

Fucker is smiling, talking to someone I can't see. Tara is behind him, can see her arms around him. But who else is in there?

"I asked to meet you both in here… ."

Ravenna. What the fuck?

"Right now," Ravenna continues. "Jordy is very confused. He's going through a lot of turmoil. Despite his obsession for you, Tara, deep down, he's a very good person. I love him and I've got a plan to help him get over it."

"We want to help him, too," Tara says. " But there's something you should know that might hurt him. Frankie and I plan to get married... ."

My pounding heart drowns out the rest of the conversation. I have only two options left; death or exile.

I'm afraid to take anything other than shallow breaths, fearing a full blown panic attack, or even a heart attack. I take short tiny puffs of the fetid bathroom air as I slowly lower myself away from the peephole, down to the damp grungy floor. I lay my head beside the filth-stained toilet base. The cool floor tiles offer relief to my burning cheek. It's comforting. I wish I could stay here forever. But, after some time, my mind clears. Thoughts come - suggestions to solve the Karpis problem.

The COMFORT of the FARM

48

I've chosen exile - fled Minneapolis for the farm.

I'm wearing dad's grease-stained coveralls - still have his smell on them. Gives me a sense of grounding.

I'm on my back, on the hard black soil - ripe golden wheat waving gently in the breeze in front of me, far as the eye can see.

No one to tell me what to do. No hassles. No headaches.

I've spent a week just wandering the farm - tramping through the barnyard grass, discovering all the junk in the woods, exploring all the various sheds - always with my screenplay in hand.

Got the lines memorized. Gotten to know Bullhead so well - acting out encounters with imagined antagonists - that I've almost become him.

A car rumbles up the long driveway, distracting me. It pulls into the yard. First visitor since I've returned. Ignore them.

Two car horn honks. Car door slams. Loud knocking on house door.

I turn over on my hands and knees and low crawl like a snake into the cover of the three-foot-tall wheat and then roll over on my back and lay looking up at the infinite blue sky, cotton clouds drifting slowly by.

I reach up and pluck a kernel from a wheat head, peel off the chaff with my thumb nail and put the bare kernel between my teeth. It's hard. How they tested grain in the old days. Ready for harvest.

Tomorrow I'll fire-up the swather and cut the field, and then get the old Super 92 going and combine it. Then I'll get the Studebaker going and truck the grain off to the Doran elevator, just like dad used to do.

BFFs

49

I wake. Still out in the field.

It's dark.

The yard light has turned everything an eerie ectoplasmic greenish-white.

Walking back to the house, I see no signs of the visitor. But there's an envelope stuck in the outside door. I take it and go inside, grab a beer, and sit at the kitchen table. There's a handwritten note in side the envelope:

Jordy,

We are all concerned about your mental health. I called Tara today to apprise her of your situation. She wanted me to relay the message that if there is anything she can do, to please text her. I cannot stress enough the importance of you contacting one of us. It is for your own health. If we do not hear from you within the next few days I'll be forced to conclude that you have fallen into misfortune and I'll have to contact the authorities.

Love,

Ravenna

I grab my phone off top the fridge, open the fb messenger ap and text Tara:

Hi, Tara. How are you?

Wavy dots followed by immediate reply.

Hello. I'm great. Where are you?

Why great? I'm out of town.

I received a lot of birthday wishes. Are you at your father's farm?

Yes. You must be very popular.

Nope. Because of Skype and Facebook notifications. But I really enjoyed your being at the party, too.

I still want to give you a belated gift.

No, you don't need to. I'm just glad you came. To be honest, you're more excited to give me one than I am.

Why is that?

But the way you are excited makes me happy. You are one of my best friends and having you remember my birthday makes me feel lucky. I don't know why you went away without letting me know. Is there anything wrong?

I feel you are less interested in the things I do recently.

* * *

No, I feel it's great. But, has something wrong happened?

I get the impression that I'm not important to you. Am I wrong?

Nope. Just me.

I feel that ever since Frankie entered the scene you've distanced yourself from me.

You think that? Yup. A little bit. I don't want to hurt you or do something wrong.

What do you mean?

Nothing. Jordy, when we have time to talk with each other I'll talk more about it, okay?

What is it about?

It's not so important because it won't effect our friendship.

But why would it hurt me?

I was just shocked about the webcam. No, it wouldn't hurt you. But it effected me and I may hurt you.

Please tell me.

The thing you should know is that you're my best friend. And don't show any videos of me to anyone.

Of course not.

Yes, that is it. Just remember something. I'll be happy when you can do that.

I'll never show them and I feel sorry for planting the cam. Can you ever forgive me?

Of course, silly. When will you be coming back to work? We all miss you here.

Thank you, sweetie. I'm just about to start the harvest here. By myself, it'll go pretty slow.

Can I help?

Seriously?!

Of course. We're BFFs.

That would be AWESOME! I'll be combining on Saturday, if you could come out then?

Done! Send me your farm's address so I can plug it into my gps. Then I'll show up with all kinds of goodies.

You'll be a sight for sore eyes. Better go now. Got a big day tomorrow. Here's my address...

KARPIS COMBINED

50

It's a bright sunny Saturday - perfect for combining. I'm not surprised to see Karpis arrive with Tara. I'm too excited about the harvest and having her here on the farm to be angry.

I'm out in the combine when she pulls in, it's sometime around noon. She parks her green Soul near the edge of the field. They set up lawn chairs and bring out a cooler. She gets me a beer right off the bat.

Gonna be a great day.

Karpis has never seen a combine. He's wowed by its size and asks a million questions. I give him a brief tutorial and have him climb up onto the operator's platform. Tara takes out her phone and captures the moment. I let them have their fun and then get down to business.

"The sun's getting high," I say, climbing aboard the combine. "We got a lot of work to do. Better get started." I tell Karpis, "Let me take the driver's seat. I'll get us started and then let you give it a try."

"Okay, boss," getting up. We shift positions with me sitting in the driver's seat and him standing beside me, clutching the guard rail.

I pull out the choke and wake the throbbing beast - almost making Karpis shit himself.

"Hold on tight," slamming down the threshing machine control lever. I pull back the throttle and the whole machine comes alive - loud as hell, trembling, vibrating, rattling. Down below, in front of us, the pick-up auger that runs the entire width of the machine, rotates hypnotically. I press down on the clutch pedal, shift into first, and then release the clutch. The Super 92 jerks forward and then slowly advances forward toward the first row of swathed wheat.

I lower the header and start eating wheat. The machine growls as it chops and sifts and spits out golden chaff from its rear end.

Tara follows, walking along side as we crawl down the field, taking videos with her phone. Karpis, standing on the platform beside me, waves and poses. I try to keep my attention on the combining, keeping it on course, on the wheat rows. But then I give in to temptation and dig my own phone out and capture Tara in her sexy tight shorts and halter. Makes me feel the way I did all those years ago when Doreen ran after me while I was sitting in this very same seat.

Since I neglected to spray the crop with herbicide back in May, the field is infested with dreaded cockle burs, wild sunflowers, thistles, and mustard plants. They make the machine hiccup and growl - forcing me to step on the clutch to avoid plug-ups.

CRUNCH!!!

The combine chokes on a huge cockle bur - stopping the threshing mechanism. Pullies screech as they turn against stuck belts, fouling the air with the smell of burning rubber.

"FUCK!" stepping on the clutch and pulling up the threshing lever.

"Is it broken?" Karpis says, disappointed look on his face.

"Can you fix it?" Tara says, walking over to the combine.

"It's just plugged up. Karpis, see all that wheat bunched up on the head?" pointing down front.

"Yes, boss," nodding enthusiastically.

"Go down and pull it out. Then I'll run what's still inside through the machine and clean it out."

"Is it safe," Tara asks.

"Yeah, the engine's running but the threshing mechanism's out of gear. Now get down there. We've got a lot a work to do."

"Okay, boss," climbing down the ladder, and walking around front. He leans into the header and starts pulling out jammed-up wheat stalks. Tara starts to move in as if to help out. "Tara, please, let him do it. Those wheat stalks are sharp and they itch. I couldn't live with myself if you got a rash."

"Ooh, good call," backing off. "Be careful, Ding, honey. Do you want some gloves?"

"It shouldn't take that long," grabbing my phone. She's so damn hot, I have to get more video of her - can't resist capturing her every curve.

It doesn't take long for Karpis to clean out the header.

"Good enough, boss?" stepping back from the header, straightening up and smiling up at me, all sweaty and caked with bits of straw.

"Let me try it." I push down the threshing lever. Pullies screech on stuck drive belts. "No go," letting up the threshing lever. "Reach deeper in between the auger teeth and pull out more straw."

"Go ahead, Frankie. Be careful," biting her lower lip as she watches him crawl up onto the header and stick his head and arms into the opening where the wheat enters the combine. I briefly capture him on video and then pan back to Tara, zooming in on her.

Peering into my phone screen, I see a figure emerge out of

the woods in the distance behind Tara.

Ravenna? What the fuck?

The witch, she's looking straight at me, flashing weird signals and signs at me with her hands, things I saw her do back during our sex magick sessions.

I fall against the threshing lever. The front auger slips, jolting the machine as it starts full bore.

"HELP!!!" Karpis screams seconds before his head is devoured.

I drop my phone and, in a panic, fumble with the levers.

Tara screams wildly up at me.

Blood spraying everywhere.

THUNK!!!

Bone fragments from inside the machine are augered into the seed hopper behind me, pelting its sheet metal sides like hail stones.

I finally manage to release the threshing lever, stopping the machine.

Tara faints.

I jump down, pick her up and carry her to the house, kick open the door, and take her to my grandparent's old bedroom - it's been preserved just as they had it forty years back; original antique furniture and bed. I lay her gently onto the made bed with religious reverence.

I tenderly kiss her lips.

Her eye lashes flutter and her lids open. A subtle smile graces her lips.

"Jordy," she moans, looking dreamily into my eyes. "Where am I?"

"You're safe, in my grandparent's house. I'll take care of you. Try to sleep. You need rest."

I'm distracted by the sound of footsteps entering the house. Turning my head, I see Ravenna stop in the bedroom doorway.

Brian Zluticky

THESE ARE MINE

51

I collapse into Ravenna's arms, worn out from our intense lovemaking. We stand holding each other in silent embrace, hanging onto each other in the deep blue velvety dark. Time has drifted away into nothingness. Until... the realization of what's happened hits me.

My breath is jagged, short, shallow.

Ravenna tilts my head back and kisses me tenderly on the lips.

I hear something.

"What's that?" I breath through our kiss.

"What's what?" Breathing back.

"Listen," dropping my head on her shoulder and being as silent as I can. "Hear it?"

She listens, too.

"You mean that tapping? That's just the wind blowing the screen door. I forgot to latch it when I came in," kissing the top of my head.

"No," lifting my head and looking toward the living room through the bedroom doorway. "Someone's knocking on the front door. I'm positive. Check the window."

I take her hand and lead her out into the living room and over to the window that looks out onto the front yard.

"You look."

She parts the curtains just a crack and peers through.

"See anything?"

"No, not from this angle," pulling back from the curtains.

"Let me see," moving to the far end of the curtains and peeking out at a more oblique angle. Dusk has fallen. The sunken sun has left an orange-brown after-burn behind the western grove. "Shit. I knew it. It ain't the wind. The trees aren't moving… and there's that tapping again. It's the cops. We're trapped."

"You could tell them it was an accident."

"Take it easy," stepping away from the window, turning to her and taking her hands. "I know a way out. Come in here," pulling her into the crudely furnished pioneer bathroom.

"What are you going to do, hide out in here?"

Mirrors, according to one remote culture are considered an abomination because they simulate the universe and confound the truth.

Entering the bathroom, I happened to catch a sideways glance of my back falsely reproduced in the smudgy-cloudy mirror above the sink. I didn't flip the light switch for fear of the cops taking notice. So what I saw was by the fading illumination of the orange dusk weakly wafting through the lone un-curtained bathroom window, its age-old glass bearing the residue of countless years of rain, snow, and wind.

I'm wearing my high school wrestling practice shirt. It has *RABNOW* silkscreened across its shoulders in bold green caps. But what the mirror shows me is *WONDAR*. WONDER? Is that another me? Jordy Wonder? *No*, my inner voice says. *Johnny Wonder*. My subconscious alter ego. The real, true me.

A feeling bordering on bliss washes over me. For the first time, in my entire life, I feel that I'm in control - totally free. I am me and not someone else's version of me.

"Baby," grabbing Ravenna by her arms and gripping her tight. "It's hard for me to do this after all we've been through and all you've done for me." She gives me a queer look, as if to ask what's gotten into me. ""But I've got new plans and I need you to fade away. Tara and me need to be alone."

"Ha!" peeling my hands off her and reaching down and grabbing my nuts. "These are mine. You murdered someone out there in that field. You need me," the fury rising in her voice.

"He was an illegal alien living under a fake name. No documentation. No one can prove he ever existed over here," grabbing the wrist of her hand clutching my balls. I vice-grip her. She releases her hold.

"You were nothing but a broke homeless hick… ," her voice pleading and laced with pain as I squeeze harder and harder. "When I picked you up off the streets. I nursed you back to health and helped you finish your screenplay," a tear running down her cheek.

"It ain't finished yet," dropping her wrist and grabbing her neck with both hands. I press my mouth to hers - squeezing, pressing my thumbs into her throat. She claws at my hands and kicks my shins with her shiny black pumps.

After a minute, I pull out of the kiss and gaze into her bulging steel-grey eyes as my thumbs press deeper into the hollow of her neck.

"I appreciate all you've done for me, Mandy." She's loosing strength and gasping, her jaws open wide as a barn door, feebly gasping. "But that was the old me." Her body goes limp. I hold her, keep her from collapsing. But I can tell she's clinging to the smallest sliver of consciousness. "Under that rug," nodding to the dirty white 2'x4' shag rug at our feet. "There's a trap door to the root cellar. In it there's an escape tunnel for you."

"I love you," the words sapping the last of her strength.

"I don't have a definition for love," kicking the rug aside.

Bending down, Ravenna's limp body falls across my right shoulder. I grab the fist-sized rusty iron ring inset into the lower right corner of the three-foot-square section of the green linoleum-covered floor. I tug up on the ring and pull up the trap door, swinging it up in an arc on its hinges till it falls back, supported by a length of rusty link chain.

My last recollection is hearing the living room linoleum creak.

Leaning forward to drop Ravenna down, I loose balance and we both tumble down the seven brutal plank steps and splash onto the water-covered cellar floor, hitting hard concrete. The trapdoor slams. Everything goes dark.

OUR LITTLE SECRET

52

He opens his eyes and lifts his head out of his hands, still sitting on the steps, dripping wet in a cold dark cellar.

A shiver shakes his chest. He tries to suppress it, gritting his teeth.

Another shiver and another. He rubs his arms and takes a deep jagged breath.

"Relax. Relax. You're okay. You're okay."

There's a dead body on the floor. Another out in the field. Tara is upstairs. When she wakes she'll freak... wait. Who pushed us down here? Tara.

"What am I going to do?" softly, almost in tears. "STOP THAT SHIT," shouting. "You know what to do. You're fucking Johnny Wonder. Go upstairs. Get dressed. Clean up the mess at the combine. Have some breakfast and... . What day is it? Sunday? Must be. Go to church like the righteous person you are. Then come back and finish the harvest, just like dad would want. You can do this. You can do this, now... because you're Johnny Wonder - just our little secret. Go ahead, let people believe you're still Jordy Rabnow if they want. You can live with that. But, first thing, go check on Tara."

He grabs hold of the 4"x4" floor-to-ceiling post standing by his knees and pulls himself up. He pivots around and climbs the steps, having to stoop to avoid hitting his head on the approaching trapdoor. He climbs three steps and presses his hands up against the rough old planks of the underside of the trapdoor. It feels heavy.

She must have put the oak chair over it.

Giving it a little of a shove, it opens up a few inches, the dim grey light of dawn washing over his face. He lifts the door a little higher and slips his hand through the opening, reaches around and grabs a chair leg to keep it from falling. He lifts the door higher and crawls up and out into the bathroom, closing the trapdoor back down behind him.

SUNNY NEW DAY

53

He hobbles into the bedroom, pulls off his wet t-shirt and stumbles into bed - feels so good. He cuddles up behind the nude body stretched out on its side, soft slender ass facing him, head buried under a pillow.

It moans and stirs.

"Saw your screenplay," it murmurs, half awake. "Up all night with it."

He sees his *Bullhead* manuscript on the nightstand across the bed. The first golden rays of dawn shine through the bedroom's east windows. Her taught smooth flesh gleams like Chinese porcelain. The room smells of her scent, reminds him of Doreen's - bombyx and moth wings and musky moldy leaves. He has an erection. Time to finally consumate their relationship. But first he needs to hear her thoughts on his story.

"So, what did you think about *Bullhead*?"

"I noticed you wrote me into it."

"And?" reaching up and lifting the pillow just a little. Enough for him to see her wide smile and to gaze into he glazed eye.

"There are certain things about me that you have to get right. But I'll help you with that."

"Baby, you don't know how happy it makes me to hear that," sliding my hand down between her thighs.

The sun pokes up above the horizon, filling the room with golden beams. She turns and wraps and an arm and a leg over him.

"Ravenna!?"

"Yes, dear," kissing him. "You're cold as ice and all wet. Here, let me warm you," rubbing against him.

He pushes her away and sits up, swinging his feet down onto the floor. Drops his head into his hands, confused.

"Tara?" he asks.

"In the cellar."

He gets up, picks up his blood-stained Levi's from off the floor and pulls them on. Grabs a denim work shirt from the closet. Puts it on and staggers out to the bathroom, sobbing.

Ravenna pulls on tight jeans and a pink tank and intercepts him, walking him out into the kitchen. Through the north window he can see Tara's green KIA Soul parked in the distance, the Super 92 beyond it.

Rage boils up inside him. He eyes a sickle lying on the table. She sees him eye it and wraps her arms tight around him from behind.

"I know," whispering in his ear. "You want to be Jordy Rabnow, America's Next Great Psychopath. But I got higher aspirations for you. I need to give you your next therapy session. Do you feel up to it?"

""I'm really tired."

"You can rest in my car. I got it parked in the grove."

She kisses him. Then slowly turns and guides him to the house's front door. She opens it onto a beautiful sunny new day.

**Read on for the first thrilling chapter from Brian Zluticky's sequel to Bullhead,
Fear and Wonder**

1

We're somewhere past Barnesville, on the edge of the hills, when the anxiety grabs. Wrap my calfskin jacket tight to fight off the chills. It's twilight time. Just before the dawn.

We slug it up the crest of the first hill when on the horizon I see this fucking three-armed giant waving his arms, beckoning us back. Turn around before it's too late.

"Shoot the fucker," grabbing the Winchester .30-30, I lean out the window and fire off round after round at the bastard. Does no good. "Got a rocket launcher back there?"

"Wake up you crazy son-of-a-bitch," Hemi says, driving one-handed and pulling me back in by the collar. "It's a fucking wind generator."

"That's what you think," jabbing the rifle in his ribs.

"Vennie, pause your prayers and grab us a couple beers," he says, flicking the barrel away like a fly.

Ravenna, sitting lotus-style on a pile of blankets behind the front seats, steps down off Mount Carmel. She opens the coffin lid, reaches her long arm in, grabs two Hamms from the ice, and lets the lid slam.

"Accipite et bibite ex eo omnes," she chants, making the sign of the cross over the dripping cans as she hands them up.

Hemi takes one, pops it, slurps it.

"Have a beer," he tells me.

"I quit."

"Have one. Do you some good."

"Too cold for beer. Got any whiskey back there?"

"There's hot herbal tea in the thermos," Ravenna says, setting the refused beer down on the console between the seats.

"Naw, I need the whiskey," teeth clattering. I exchange the rifle for the pint and take a shot. Heats up the gut and chases back the chills. I lean back and watch the two-lane blacktop scroll beneath us. The horizon is brightening behind the thing. He's right. A gawd-awful windmill. What the fuck? Is this Spain?"

We hit the next peak and several of his friends join him in the distance, spread out all along his flanks like an army of mechanical monsters... or are they watch towers?

"I don't remember those damn things being out there before. This is God's country. What's this fucking world coming to?"

"Times have changed since your last reunion."

We're in a rusty white '92 Ram Charger lugging a twenty-foot flatbed loaded with a 1934 McCormick-Derring W-30 tractor and three Arctic Cat minibikes headed for the largest display of working antique farm machinery in the known world - the steam threshers reunion up in Rollag, Minnesota.

For a lot of people Rollag would be a real wrist-slasher. But we veterans of the show know how to do it right. We got the Ram loaded with everything we need for four down-n-dirty old-timy days on the show grounds: four thirty-packs of

Hamms, four quarts of whiskey, burgers, brats, chips, a grill, lawn chairs, a four-man tent, sleeping bags, warm jackets for the cool early September nights, bottle rockets, a fully stocked tool chest, flashlights,… and a dead body.

Fuck! Excuse these chills. Take another shot of whiskey.

When we were kids, Hemi and me and our dad and our uncle, all hit the reunion every year (hell, even goes back before that - got a pic of us there with gramps when I was just three and Hemi one). We all took tractors and drove em in the parade. The best of times. Want to share em with Ravenna (friend, therapist, renegade nun who has the hots for me - couldn't shake her from tagging along), her first time.

We got up at zero-dark-thirty to make the one-hour haul up from New Manchuria. Get there when the gates open at six. Beat the crowds. Get a good camping spot. Not have to wait in a gawd-awful long line for thresherman's breakfast.

Turning onto State HWY 32, we head due north. After a few rolling hills of wheat and corn, we pass through the quiet town of Rollag: just a cluster of simple old houses, a machine shop, an old country store, and a little white church. We breeze through in five seconds flat and come to the intersection of a gravel road.

Our first sight of the promised land. A carpet of cars glitters in a stubble-field parking lot. Half a mile beyond, blanketed in sun-kissed steam and smoke, is Steamer Hill. A panoply of pennants, bearing the insignias of defunct tractor companies, marks the exhibit grounds filled with row after row of old tractors.

"Looks like some Dante-esque mechanical hell," Ravenna says. "What's with all the smoke?"

"They're firing up the steamers!"

"Well, could you at least roll up your window, please," covering her nose with her shawl.

"Fuck that," Hemi says, inhaling deeply. "Ahhh, paradise."

Planted in the front yard of the last house in town is a billboard with a picture of a threshing rig. Giant chopstick script proclaims:

CHAIRMAN MAO'S MEMORIAL
STEAM THRESHERS REUNION
WORKERS DAY WEEKEND
SEPTEMBER 1, 2, 3, & 4

At the bottom of the sign, the ominous line:

SPONSORED by the CHINESE OCCUPATION
GOVERNMENT
PRESERVING YOUR AMERICAN HERITAGE

I rub my eyes and look again. Am I awake? Did I really see that? "Do you see that?" pointing it out to Hemi.

"Fucking-A right," he says, slowing to make a right at the intersection. "Look at this asshole."

A biker with an orange safety vest over his greasy road gear is beckoning us forward with a circular motion of his hand while pointing a cane up the gravel road. Like, duh, motherfucker. He's a member of the BROFOS - a Christian motorcycle club out of New Manchuria. Recently had a run-in with one of their members, so I don't want him to recognize me. I slouch down, we turn, and get by without incident. Thank God he didn't recognize the minibikes.

Half a mile up the dusty road another biker waves us into the workers/campers entrance. We turn in and pull up to a ticket shack just inside the chainlink fence.

A freckle-faced doe-eyed girl in bib overalls and an engineer's cap strolls over from the shack up to Hemi's window. A show button featuring a bright red antique tractor proclaims *MASSEY HARRIS EXTRAVAGANZA*. It's pinned to the side of her cap. Below the button hang two ribbons spread at a thirty degree angle - one black, one white. The white one says *MEMBER*. The black one says *WORKER*.

"Hi, there," she says, sweet as morning dew, grinning wide.

"Mornin, pumpkin puss," Hemi says. "We're workers here to drop off an exhibit," hitching his thumb over his shoulder at the W-30. He guns the engine and rolls forward.

"Whoa, whoa," she says, jogging up to the Ram.

Hemi eases off the gas.

"Ah, are those vintage minibikes," her eyes popping. "They are, aren't they? Way cool!"

"Want to ride one," Hemi stops, flashing a wolfish grin. He gulps his beer to the dregs, crushes the can, and drops it jangling at his feet. "How old are you? Eighteen?"

"I'm fourteen. But I can drive steamers," nodding eagerly.

"Well, hop on in."

"I've got to stay here till nine. Do you have your gate passes yet?"

"Like I said, we're workers. We'll get em up at the Hiterdall Depot."

"They don't give them there. You have to get them here. Three season passes will be sixty dollars, please."

"Thought workers got in free."

"Nope. Everyone has to pay," holding out her tender hand.

"Shit, we ain't got that much," looking at me and then back at Ravenna. "Well, ah, Vennie, maybe you ought to talk to this girl."

"Good idea," she says, leaning forward, wedging her narrow face out the narrow space between the back of Hemi's seat's headrest and the driver's window. She smiles warmly and says, "There's something very important you should know about our weekend here."

The girl's wide grin shrivels to polite concern.

A huge shambling, rumbling, snorting, popping Oilpull tractor lumbers across our path twenty feet ahead. Fills the air with the mind-altering effluvium of kerosine and oil. We pause as all eyes turn in reverence to the godly machine. It takes its time crawling by.

Ravenna shouts above the noise, "We're on a special mission... to find the cure for the American Dream."

"You get that?" Hemi shouts in the girl's face.

"What?" shaking her head, cupping her ear, confused look in her eyes.

"Let me try," leaning over sideways between Hemi and the steering wheel. "We're on a grave venture, here. At this very moment I, myself, am experiencing deep despair along with certain premonitions which may or may not be suicidal tendencies," clasping my left hand on Hemi's shoulder. "This sweet guy here is my brother. And," letting my hand fall down onto Ravenna's slender knee. "This pious woman woman is my therapist. They've come along merely just to try and keep me alive."

The smile falls from the girl's lips. She turns her head and looks back at the ticket shack where an old duffer is selling passes to walk-ins. She shoots a glance over at the biker directing traffic some hundred feet back. Cars and pickups are piling up behind us. The girl turns her attention back to us, uncertain as to what to do.

My left hand leaves Ravenna's knee and finds the earlier refused can of Hamms sitting between the seats. I pick it up and hold it out to her, "Here, looks like you could use this."

"Alcoholic beverages are not allowed on the show grounds," thunder clouds forming over those doe eyes.

"It's alright," Ravenna says. "He has a doctor's prescription for it. Helps medicate his extreme state of anxiety."

The girl is completely flummoxed. She realizes the only

way to get rid of us is to just give us our passes and let us in.

"We're really not like all the others," I say, giving her sad puppy eyes. "We're just trying to find the lost art of what it means to be truly human… eternal souls are at stake here."

Hemi grabs the twice rejected Hamms, pops it, spilling suds on his vintage Arctic Cat jacket, and takes a gulp. "Got a map showing the nearest outhouse? Got a piss something fierce."

His vulgarity trumps her indecision. She steps back to the shack, grabs a sheet of paper from a stack off the ledge and brings it back. It's a printout map of the show grounds. She takes a yellow highlighter from a narrow pencil pocket in her bib and makes a circle on the map. Hands Hemi the map, trace of disgust pulling her lips.

"I'll consider you a special case and let you in," digging in her hip pocket, she pulls out three pink bracelet passes. "Here, you can wear these," handing then in the window.

"Keep that faggot shit, honey," Hemi says, shifting into drive and creeping forward.

"Bless you, my child," Ravenna says, making the sign of the cross to her. "In nominee Patris, et Filii, et Spiritus Sancti."

We hang a left just inside the fence. A posted sign says:

WARNING:
IN THE SPIRIT OF THE SHOW
ALL MICROWAVE COMMUNICATION
HAS BEEN BLOCKED

We all check our cell phones. No bars all around.

"Fuck it," Hemi says. "We don't need no stinking 911."

We should have turned back.

www.ingramcontent.com/pod-product-compliance
Lightning Source LLC
Chambersburg PA
CBHW071235130626
46556CB00003B/1024